Sonny
A Christmas Guest

Ruth McEnery Stuart

SONNY A CHRISTMAS GUEST

A boy, you say, doctor? An' she don't know it yet? Then what 're you tellin' me for? No, sir—takes it away. I don't want to lay my eyes on it till she's saw it—not if I am its father. She's its mother, I reckon!

Better lay it down somew'eres an' go to her—not there on the rockin'-cheer, for somebody to set on—'n' not on the trunk, please. That ain't none o' yo' ord'nary new-born bundles, to be dumped on a box that'll maybe be opened sudden d'rec'ly for somethin' needed, an' be dropped ag'in' the wall-paper behind it.

It's hers, whether she knows it or not. Don't, for gracious sakes, lay 'im on the table! Anybody knows that's bad luck.

You think it might bother her on the bed? She's that bad? An' they ain't no fire kindled in the settin'-room, to lay it in there.

S-i-r? Well, yas, I—I reck'n I'll haf to hold it, ef you say so—that is—of co'se—

Wait, doctor! Don't let go of it yet! Lordy! but I'm thess shore to drop it! Lemme set down first, doctor, here by the fire an' git het th'ugh. Not yet! My ol' shin-bones stan' up thess like a pair o' dog-irons. Lemme bridge 'em over first 'th somethin' soft. That'll do. She patched that quilt herself. Hold on a minute, 'tel I git the aidges of it under my ol' boots, to keep it fom saggin' down in the middle.

There, now! Merciful goodness, but I never! I'd rather trus' myself with a whole playin' fountain in blowed glass'n sech ez this.

Stoop down there, doctor, please, sir, an' shove the end o' this quilt a leetle further under my foot, won't you? Ef it was to let up sudden, I wouldn't have no more lap 'n what any other fool man's got.

'N' now—you go to her.

I'd feel a heap safer ef this quilt was nailed to the flo' on each side o'my legs. They're trimblin' so I dunno what minute my feet'll let go their holt.

An' she don't know it yet! An' he layin' here, dressed up in all the little clo'es she sewed! She mus' be purty bad. I dunno, though; maybe that's gen'ally the way.

They're keepin' mighty still in that room. Blessed ef I don't begin to feel 'is warmth in my ol' knee-bones! An' he's a-breathin' thess ez reg'lar ez that clock, on'y quicker. Lordy! An' she don't know it yet! An' he a boy! He taken that after the Joneses; we've all been boys in our male branch. When that name strikes, seem like it comes to stay. Now for a girl—

Wonder if he ain't covered up mos' too close-t. Seem like he snuffles purty loud—for a beginner.

Doctor! oh, doctor! I say, doctor!

Strange he don't hear—'n' I don't like to holler no louder. Wonder ef she could be worse? Ef I could thess reach somethin' to knock with! I daresn't lif' my foot, less'n the whole business'd fall through.

Oh, doc'! Here he comes now—Doctor, I say, don't you think maybe he's covered up too—

How's she, doctor? "Thess the same," you say? 'n' she don't know yet—about him? "In a couple o' hours," you say? Well, don't lemme keep you, doctor. But, tell me, don't you think maybe he's covered up a leetle too close-t?

That's better. An' now I've saw him befo' she did! An' I didn't want to, neither.

Poor leetle, teenchy, weenchy bit of a thing! Ef he ain't the very littlest! Lordy, Lordy, Lordy! But I s'pose all thet's needed in a baby is a startin'-p'int big enough to hol' the fam'ly ch'racteristics. I s'pose maybe he is, but the po' little thing mus' feel sort o' scrouged with 'em, ef he's got 'em all—the Joneses' an' the Simses'. Seem to me he favors her a little thess aroun' the mouth.

An' she don't know it yet!

'Seem to me he favors her a little thess aroun' the mouth.'
'Seem to me he favors her a little thess aroun' the mouth.'

Lord! But my legs ache like ez if they was bein' wrenched off. I've got 'em on sech a strain, somehow. An' he on'y a half hour ol', an' two hours mo' 'fo' I can budge! Lord, Lord! how will I stand it!

God bless 'im! Doc! He's a-sneezin'! Come quick! Shore ez I'm here, he snez twice-t!

Don't you reckon you better pile some mo' wood on the fire an'—

What's that you say? "Fetch 'im along"? An' has she ast for 'im? Bless the Lord! I say. But a couple of you 'll have to come help me loosen up 'fo' I can stir, doctor.

Here, you stan' on that side the quilt, whiles I stir my foot to the flo' where it won't slip—an' Dicey—where's that nigger Dicey? You Dicey, come on here, an' tromp on the other side o' this bedquilt till I h'ist yo' young marster up on to my shoulder.

No, you don't take 'im, neither. I'll tote 'im myself.

Now, go fetch a piller till I lay 'im on it. That's it. And now git me somethin' stiff to lay the piller on. There! That lapboa'd 'll do. Why didn't I think about that befo'? It's a heap safeter 'n my ole knee-j'ints. Now, I've got 'im secure. Wait, doctor—hold on! I'm afeered you 'll haf to ca'y 'im in to her, after all. I'll cry ef I do it. I'm trimblin' like ez ef I had a'ager, thess a-startin' in with 'im—an seein' me give way might make her nervous. You take 'im to her, and lemme come in sort o' unconcerned terreckly, after she an' him've kind o' got acquainted. Dast you hold 'im that-a-way, doctor, 'thout no support to 'is spinal colume? I s'pose he is too sof' to snap, but I wouldn't resk it. Reckon I can slip in the other do' where she won't see me, an' view the meetin'.

Yas; I 'm right here, honey! (The idea o' her a-callin' for me—an' him in 'er arms!) I 'm right here, honey—mother! Don't min' me a-cryin'! I'm all broke up, somehow; but don't you fret. I 'm right here by yo' side on my knees, in pure thankfulness.

Bless His name, I say! You know he's a boy, don't yer? I been a holdin' 'im all day—'t least ever sence they dressed 'im, purty nigh a' hour ago. An' he's slep'—an' waked up—an' yawned—an' snez—an' wunk—an' sniffed—'thout me sayin' a word. Opened an' shet his little fist, once-t, like ez ef he craved to shake hands, howdy! He cert'n'y does perform 'is functions wonderful.

Yas, doctor; I'm a-comin', right now.

Go to sleep now, honey, you an' him, an' I'll be right on the spot when needed. Lemme whisper to her thess a minute, doctor?

I thess want to tell you, honey, thet you never, even in yo' young days, looked ez purty to my eyes ez what you do right now. An' that boy is yo' boy, an' I ain't a-goin' to lay no mo' claim to 'im 'n to see thet you have yo' way with 'im—you hear? An' now good night, honey, an' go to sleep.

They wasn't nothin' lef for me to do but to come out here in this ol' woodshed where nobody wouldn't see me ac' like a plumb baby.

An' now, seem like I can't git over it! The idee o' me, fifty year ol', actin' like this!

An' she knows it! An' she's got 'im—a boy—layin' in the bed 'longside 'er.

"Mother an' child doin' well!" Lord, Lord! How often I've heerd that said! But it never give me the all-overs like it does now, some way.

Guess I'll gether up a' armful o' wood, an' try to act unconcerned—an' laws-a-mercy me! Ef—to-day—ain't—been—Christmas! My! my! my! An' it come an' gone befo' I remembered!

I'll haf to lay this wood down ag'in an' think.

I've had many a welcome Christmas gif' in my life, but the idee o' the good Lord a-timin' this like that!

Christmas! An' a boy! An' she doin' well!

No wonder that ol' turkey-gobbler sets up on them rafters blinkin' at me so peaceful! He knows he's done passed a critical time o' life.

You've done crossed another bridge safe-t, ol' gobbly, an' you can afford to blink—an' to set out in the clair moonlight, 'stid o' roostin' back in the shadders, same ez you been doin'.

You was to 've died by ax-ident las' night, but the new visitor thet's dropped in on us ain't cut 'is turkey teeth yet, an' his mother—

Lord, how that name sounds! Mother! I hardly know 'er by it, long ez I been tryin' to fit it to 'er—an' fearin' to, too, less'n somethin' might go wrong with either one.

I even been callin' him "it" to myself all along, so 'feerd thet ef I set my min' on either the "he" or the "she" the other one might take a notion to come—an' I didn't want any disappointment mixed in with the arrival.

But now he's come,—an' registered, ez they say at the polls,—I know I sort o' counted on the boy, some way.

Lordy! but he's little! Ef he hadn't 'a' showed up so many of his functions spontaneous, I'd be oneasy less'n he mightn't have 'em; but they're there! Bless goodness, they're there!

An' he snez prezac'ly, for all the world, like my po' ol' pap—a reg'lar little cat sneeze, thess like all the Joneses.

Well, Mr. Turkey, befo' I go back into the house, I'm a-goin' to make you a solemn promise.

You go free till about this time next year, anyhow. You an' me'll celebrate the birthday between ourselves with that contrac'. You needn't git oneasy Thanksgivin', or picnic-time, or Easter, or no other time 'twixt this an' nex' Christmas—less'n, of co'se, you stray off an' git stole.

An' this here reprieve, I want you to understand, is a present from the junior member of this firm.

Lord! but I'm that tickled! This here wood ain't much needed in the house,—the wood-boxes 're all full,—but I can't devise no other excuse for vacatin'—thess at this time.

S'pose I might gether up some eggs out 'n the nestes, but it'd look sort o' flighty to go egg-huntin' here at midnight—an' he not two hours ol'.

I dunno, either, come to think; she might need a new-laid egg—sof b'iled. Reckon I'll take a couple in my hands—an' one or two sticks o' wood—an' I'll draw a bucket o' water too—an' tote that in.

Goodness! but this back yard is bright ez day! Goin' to be a clair, cool night— moon out, full an' white. Ef this ain't the stillest stillness!

Thess sech a night, for all the world, I reckon, ez the first Christmas, when He come—

When shepherds watched their flocks by night,
  All seated on the ground,
The angel o' the Lord come down,
  An' glory shone around—

thess like the hymn says.

The whole o' this back yard is full o' glory this minute. Th' ain't nothin' too low down an' mean for it to shine on, neither—not even the well-pump or the cattle-trough—'r the pig-pen—or even me.

Thess look at me, covered over with it! An' how it does shine on the roof o' the house where they lay—her an' him!

I suppose that roof has shined that-a-way frosty nights 'fo' to-night; but some way I never seemed to see it.

Don't reckon the creakin' o' this windlass could disturb her—or him.

Reckon I might go turn a little mo' cotton-seed in the troughs for them cows— an' put some extry oats out for the mules an' the doctor's mare—an' onchain Rover, an' let 'im stretch 'is legs a little. I'd like everything on the place to know he's come, an' to feel the diff'ence.

Well, now I'll load up—an' I do hope nobody won't notice the redic'lousness of it.

You say she's asleep, doctor, an' th' ain't nothin' mo' needed to be did—an' yo' 're goin'!

Don't, for gracious sakes! go, doctor, an' leave me! I wont know what on top o' the round earth to do, ef—ef—You know she—she might wake up—or he!

You say Dicey she knows. But she's on'y a nigger, doctor. Yes; I know she's had exper'ence with the common run o' babies, but—

Lemme go an' set down this bucket, an' lay this stick o' wood on the fire, an' put these eggs down, so's I can talk to you free-handed.

Step here to the do', doctor. I say, doc, ef it's a question o' the size o' yo' bill, you can make it out to suit yo'self—or, I'll tell you what I'll do. You stay right along here a day or so—tell to-morrer or nex' day, anyhow—an' I'll sen' you a whole bale o' cotton—an' you can sen' back any change you see fit—or none— or none, I say. Or, ef you'd ruther take it out in pertaters an' corn an' sorghum, thess say so, an' how much of each.

But what? "It wouldn't be right? Th' ain't no use," you say? An' you'll shore come back to-morrer? Well. But, by the way, doctor, did you know to-day was Christmas? Of co'se I might've knew you did—but I never. An' now it seems to me like Christmas, an' Fo'th o' July, an' "Hail Columbia, happy lan'," all b'iled down into one big jubilee!

But tell me, doctor, confidential—sh!—step here a leetle further back—tell me, don't you think he's to say a leetle bit undersized? Speak out, ef he is.

Wh—how'd you say? "Mejum," eh? Thess mejum! An' they do come even littler yet? An' you say mejum babies're thess ez liable to turn out likely an' strong ez over-sizes, eh? Mh-hm! Well, I reckon you know—an' maybe the less they have to contend with at the start the better.

Oh, thanky, doctor! Don't be afeered o' wrenchin' my wris'! A thousand thankies! Yo' word for it, he's a fine boy! An' you've inspected a good many, an' of co'se you know—yas, yas! Shake ez hard ez you like—up an' down—up an' down!

An' now I'll go git yo' horse—an' don't ride 'er too hard to-night, 'cause I've put a double po'tion of oats in her trough awhile ago. The junior member he give instructions that everything on the place was to have a' extry feed to-night—an' of co'se I went and obeyed orders.

Now—'fo' you start, doctor—I ain't got a thing stronger 'n raspberry corjal in the house—but ef you'll drink a glass o' that with me? (Of co'se he will!)

She made this 'erself, doctor—picked the berries an' all—an' I raised the little sugar thet's in it. Well, good-night, doctor! To-morrer, shore!

Sh-h!

How that do'-latch does click! Thess like thunder!

Sh-h! Dicey, you go draw yo' pallet close-t outside the do', an' lay down—an' I'll set here by the fire an' keep watch.

How my ol' stockin'-feet do tromp! Do lemme hurry an' set down! Seem like this room's awful rackety, the fire a-poppin' an' tumblin', an' me breathin' like a porpoise. Even the clock ticks ez excited ez I feel. Wonder how they sleep through it all! But they do. He beats her a-snorin' a'ready, blest ef he don't! Wonder ef he knows he's born into the world, po' little thing! I reckon not; but they's no tellin'. Maybe that's the one thing the good Lord gives 'em to know, so's they'll realize what to begin to study about—theirselves an' the world—how to fight it an' keep friends with it at the same time. Ef I could giggle an' sigh both at once-t, seem like I'd be relieved. Somehow I feel sort o' tight 'roun' the heart—an' wide awake an'—

How that clock does travel—an' how they all keep time, he—an' she—an' it—an' me—an' the fire roa'in' up the chimbley, playin' a tune all around us like a' organ, an' he—an' she—an' he—an' it—an' he—an'—

Blest ef I don't hear singing—an' how white the moonlight is! They's angels all over the house—-an' their robes is breshin' the roof whilst they sing—

His head had fallen. He was dreaming.

THE BOY

Here's the doctor, now! Hello, Doc, come right in! Here's yo' patient, settin' up on the po'ch, big ez life; but when we sent for you this mornin' it seemed thess hit an' miss whether he'd come thoo or not.

Thess the same sort o' spells he's had all along, doctor,—seems you can't never see 'im in one,—all brought on by us a-crossin' 'im. His gran'ma insisted on hidin' the clock when he wanted it; but I reckon she'll hardly resk it ag'in, she's that skeert. He's been settin' on the flo' there thess the way you see 'im now, with that clock in his lap, all mornin'.

Of co'se it thess took him about ten minutes to bu'st all the little things his gran'ma give him to play with, 'n' then he nachelly called for the clock; 'n' when she wasn't forthcomin' immejate, why, he thess stiffened out in a spell.

Of co'se we put the timepiece into his hands quick ez we could onclinch 'em, an' sent for you. But quick ez he see the clock, he come thoo. But you was already gone for, then.

His gran'ma she got considerable fretted because he's broke off the long han' o' the clock; but I don't see much out o' the way about that. Ef a person thess remembers thet the long han' is the short han'—why, 't ain't no trouble.

An' she does make 'im so contented an' happy! Thess look at his face, now! What is the face-vally of a clock, I like to know, compared to that?

'Quick ez he see the clock, he come thoo.'
'Quick ez he see the clock, he come thoo.'
But of co'se the ol' lady she's gettin' on in years, and then she's my wife's mother, which makes her my direc' mother-in-law; an' so I'm slow to conterdic' anything she says, an' I guess her idees o' regulatin' childern—not to say clocks—is sort o' diff'rent to wife's an' mine. She goes in for reg'lar discipline, same ez she got an' survived in her day; an' of co'se, ez Sonny come to her ez gran'son the same day he was born to us ez plain son, we never like to lift our voices ag'in anything she says.

She loves him thess ez well ez we do, only on a diff'rent plan. She give him the only spankin' he's ever had—an' the only silver cup.

Even wife an' me we had diff'rent idees on the subjec' o' Sonny's raisin'; but somehow, in all our ca'culations, we never seemed to realize that he'd have idees.

Why, that two-year-old boy settin' there regulatin' that clock warn't no mo' 'n to say a pink spot on the piller 'fo' he commenced to set fo'th his idees, and he ain't never backed down on no principle thet he set fo'th, to this day.

For example, wife an' me, why, we argued back an' fo'th consider'ble on the subjec' of his meal-hours, ez you might say, she contendin' for promiskyus refreshment an' me for schedule time.

This, of co'se, was thess projeckin' 'fo' the new boa'der ac-chilly arrived, He not bein' here yet, we didn't have much to do but speculate about him. Lookin' back'ards now, it seems to me we couldn't'a' had nothin' to do, day or night, 'fo' he come.

But, ez I was sayin', she was for meals at all hours, an' I was for the twenty-minutes-for-refreshment plan, an' we discussed it consider'ble, me always knowin', but never lettin' on, thet of co'se she, havin' what you might call a molopoly on the restaurant, could easy have things her own way, ef she'd choose.

But, sir, from the time he looked over that bill o' fare an' put his finger on what he'd have, an' when, that boy ain't never failed to call for it, an' get it, day 'r night.

But, talkin' 'bout the clock, it did seem funny for him to keep her goin' 'thout no key.

But somehow he'd work it thet that alarm 'd go off in the dead hours o' night, key or no key, an' her an' me we'd jump out o' bed like ez ef we was shot; and do you b'lieve thet that baby, not able to talk, an' havin' on'y half 'is teeth, he ain't never failed to wake up an' roa' out a-laughin' ever' time that clock 'd go off in the night!

Why, sir, it's worked on me so, sometimes, thet I've broke out in a col' sweat, an' set up the balance o' the night—an' I ain't to say high-strung, neither.

No, sir, we ain't never named 'im yet. Somehow, we don't seem to be able to confine ourselves to no three or four names for 'im, for so we thess decided to let it run along so—he thess goin' by the name o' "Sonny" tell sech a time ez he sees fit to name 'isself.

Of co'se I sort o' ca'culate on him takin' the "Junior," an' lettin' me tack a capital "S" an' a little "r" to my name 'fo' I die; which would nachelly call attention to him direc' eve'y time I'd sign my signature.

Deuteronomy Jones ain't to say a purty name, maybe; but it's scriptu'al—so far ez my parents could make it. Of co'se the Jones—well, they couldn't help that no mo' 'n I can help it, or Sonny, or his junior, thet, of co'se, may never be called on to appear in the flesh, Sonny not bein' quite thoo with his stomach-teeth yet, an' bein' subject to croup, both of which has snapped off many a fam'ly tree fore to-day. But I reckon the Joneses ain't suffered much that a-way. I doubt ef any of 'em has ever left 'thout passin' the name on—not knowin' positive, but thess jedgin'. None o' mine ain't, I know, leastwise none of my direc' ancestors—they couldn't have, an' me here, an' Sonny.

Don't jump, doctor! That's the supper-bell. 'Tis purty loud, but that's on account o' my mother-in-law. She's stone-deef—can't hear thunder; but I told wife thet I thought we owed it to her to do the best we could to reach her, and I had that bell made a-purpose.

Now, some men they'd slight a mother-in-law like that, an' maybe ring a dummy at her; but that's thess where I differ. I don't forget where I get my benefits, an' ef it hadn't 'a' been for her, the family circle o' Deuteronomy Jones would be quite diff'rent to what it is. She's handed down some of Sonny's best traits to him, too.

I don't say she give him his hearin', less'n she give 'm all she had—which, of co'se, I'm thess a-jokin', which is a sin, an' her stone-deef, and Sonny thess come thoo a death-spell!

Me havin' that extry sized bell made thess out of respects to her tickled her mightily.

Come along, Sonny! He heerd the bell, an' he knows what it means. That's right—fetch the clock along.

Sonny's cheer is toler'ble low, an' he's took a notion to set on the clock mealtimes. I thess lay 'er face down'ards in his cheer, 'n' I don't know ez it hurts her any; 'n' then it saves the dictionary, too.

She did strike that a-way one day, and Sonny was so tickled he purty near choked on a batter-cake, he laughed so. He has broke sev'ral casters tryin' to jostle her into doin' it again, but somehow she won't. Seem like a clock kin be about ez contrary ez anything else, once't git her back up.

He got so worked up over her not strikin' that a-way one day thet he stiffened out in a spell, then an' there.

You say they ain't apt to be fatal, doctor—them spells!

Well—but you ain't never saw him in one yet. They're reg'lar death-spells, doctor.

Tell you the truth, they was the 'casion of us j'inin' the church, them spells was.

Says I to wife—standin' beside him one day, and he black in the face—says I, "Wife," says I, "I reckon you an' me better try to live mo' righteously 'n what we've been doin', or he'll be took from us." An', sir, the very nex' communion we both up an' perfessed. An' I started sayin' grace at table, an' lef' off the on'y cuss-word I ever did use, which was "durn." An', maybe I oughtn't to say it, but I miss that word yet. I didn't often call on it, but I always knowed 't was there when needed, and it backed me up, somehow—thess the way knowin' I had a frock-coat in the press has helped me wear out ol' clo'es. I ain't never had on that frock-coat sence I was married in it seventeen year ago; but, sir, ever sence I've knew the moths had chawed it up, th' ain't been a day but I've felt shabby.

'She does make 'im so contented an' happy.'
'She does make 'im so contented an' happy.'
Sir? Yas, sir; we've waited a long time. It's seventeen year, come this spring, sence we married. Our first child could easy 'a' been sixteen year ol', 'stid o' two, ef Sonny'd come on time, but he ain't never been known to hurry hisself. But it does look like, with seventeen year for reflection, an' nothin' to do but study up other folks's mistakes with their childern, we ought to be able to raise him right. Wife an' me we fully agree upon one p'int, 'n' that is, thet mo'

childern 'r' sp'iled thoo bein' crossed an' hindered 'n any other way. Why, sir, them we 've see' grow up roun' this country hev been fed on daily rations of "dont's!" an' "stops!" an' "quits!"—an' most of 'em brought up by hand at that!

An' so, ez I say, we don't never cross Sonny, useless. Of co'se when he's been sick we have helt his little nose an' insisted on things; but I reckon we 've made it up to him afterwards, so's he wouldn't take it amiss.

Oh, yas, sir; he called me "daddy" hisself, 'n' I never learned it to him, neither. I was layin' out to learn 'im to say "papa" to me, in time; but I 'lowed I 'd hol' back tell he called her name first. Seemed like that was her right, somehow, after all thet had passed 'twixt him an' her; an' in all her baby-talk to him I took notice she'd bring the "mama" in constant.

So of co'se I laid low, hopin' some day he 'd ketch it—an' he did. He wasn't no mo' 'n 'bout three months ol' when he said it; 'n' then, 'fo' I could ketch my breath, hardly, an put in my claim, what does he do but square aroun', an', lookin' at me direc', say "dada!" thess like that.

There's the secon' bell, doctor. 'Sh! Don't ring no mo', Dicey! We're a-comin'!

At the first bell the roller-towel an' basin gen'ally holds a reception; but to-day bein' Sunday—

What? Can't stay? But you must. Quick ez Sonny come thoo this mornin', wife took to the kitchen, 'cause, she says, says she, "Likely ez not the doctor 'll miss his dinner on the road, 'n' I 'll turn in with Dicey an' see thet he makes it up on supper."

"Eat an' run?" Why not, I like to know? Come on out. Wife's at the roller-towel now, and she 'll be here in a minute.

Come on, Sonny. Let "dada" tote the clock for you. No? Wants to tote 'er hisself? Well, he shall, too.

But befo' we go out, doc, say that over ag'in, please.

Yas, I understan'. Quick ez he's took with a spell, you say, th'ow col' water in his face, an' "never min' ef he cries"!

I'll try it, doctor; but, 'twixt me an' you, I doubt ef anybody on the lot'll have the courage to douse 'im. Maybe we might call in somebody passin', an' git them to do it. But for the rest,—the bath an' the mustard,—of co'se it shall be did correct. You see, the trouble hez always been thet befo' we could git any physic measured out, he come thoo.

Many's the time that horse hez been saddled to sen' for you befo' to-day. He thess happened to get out o' sight to-day when Sonny seemed to feel the clock in his hands, an' he come thoo 'thout us givin' him anything but the clock—an' it external.

Walk out, doctor.

THE CHRISTENIN'

Yas, sir, wife an' me, we've turned 'Piscopals—all on account o' Sonny. He seemed to perfer that religion, an' of co'se we wouldn't have the family divided, so we're a-goin' to be ez good 'Piscopals ez we can.

I reckon it'll come a little bit awkward at first. Seem like I never will git so thet I can sass back in church 'thout feelin' sort o' impident—but I reckon I'll chirp up an' come to it, in time.

I never was much of a hand to sound the amens, even in our own Methodist meetin's.

Sir? How old is he? Oh, Sonny's purty nigh six—but he showed a pref'ence for the 'Piscopal Church long fo' he could talk.

When he wasn't no mo' 'n three year old we commenced a-takin' him round to church wherever they held meetin's,—'Piscopals, Methodists or Presbyterians,—so's he could see an' hear for hisself. I ca'yed him to a baptizin' over to Chinquepin Crik, once-t, when he was three. I thought I'd let him see it done an' maybe it might make a good impression; but no, sir! The Baptists didn't suit him! Cried ever' time one was douced, an' I had to fetch him away. In our Methodist meetin's he seemed to git worked up an' pervoked, some way. An' the Presbyterians, he didn't take no stock in them at all. Ricollect, one Sunday the preacher, he preached a mighty powerful disco'se on the doctrine o' lost infants not 'lected to salvation—an' Sonny? Why, he slep' right thoo it.

The first any way lively interest he ever seemed to take in religious services was at the 'Piscopals, Easter Sunday. When he seen the lilies an' the candles he thess clapped his little hands, an' time the folks commenced answerin' back he was tickled all but to death, an' started answerin' hisself—on'y, of co'se he 'd answer sort o' hit an' miss.

I see then thet Sonny was a natu'al-born 'Piscopal, an' we might ez well make up our minds to it—an' I told her so, too. They say some is born so. But we thought we'd let him alone an' let nature take its co'se for awhile—not pressin' him one way or another. He never had showed no disposition to be christened, an' ever sence the doctor tried to vaccinate him he seemed to git the notion that christenin' an' vaccination was mo' or less the same thing; an' sence that time, he's been mo' opposed to it than ever.

Sir? Oh no, sir. He didn't vaccinate him; he thess tried to do it; but Sonny, he wouldn't begin to allow it. We all tried to indoose 'im. I offered him everything on the farm ef he'd thess roll up his little sleeve an' let the doctor look at his arm—promised him thet he wouldn't tech a needle to it tell he said the word. But he wouldn't. He 'lowed thet me an' his mama could git vaccinated ef we wanted to, but he wouldn't.

Then we showed him our marks where we had been vaccinated when we was little, an' told him how it had kep' us clair o' havin' the smallpock all our lives.

Well, sir, it didn't make no diff'ence whether we'd been did befo' or not, he 'lowed thet he wanted to see us vaccinated ag'in.

An' so, of co'se, thinkin' it might encour'ge him, we thess had it did over—tryin' to coax him to consent after each one, an' makin' pertend like we enjoyed it.

Then, nothin' would do but the nigger, Dicey, had to be did, an' then he 'lowed thet he wanted the cat did, an' I tried to strike a bargain with him thet if Kitty got vaccinated he would. But he wouldn't comp'omise. He thess let on thet Kit had to be did whe'r or no. So I ast the doctor ef it would likely kill the cat, an' he said he reckoned not, though it might sicken her a little. So I told him to go ahead. Well, sir, befo' Sonny got thoo, he had had that cat an' both dogs vaccinated—but let it tech hisself he would not.

I was mighty sorry not to have it did, 'cause they was a nigger thet had the smallpock down to Cedar Branch, fifteen mile away, an' he didn't die, neither. He got well. An' they say when they git well they're more fatal to a neighborhood 'n when they die.

That was fo' months ago now, but to this day ever' time the wind blows from sou'west I feel oneasy, an' try to entice Sonny to play on the far side o' the house.

Well, sir, in about ten days after that we was the down-in-the-mouthest crowd on that farm, man an' beast, thet you ever see. Ever' last one o' them vaccinations took, sir, an' took severe, from the cat up.

But I reckon we 're all safe-t guarded now. They ain't nothin' on the place thet can fetch it to Sonny, an' I trust, with care, he may never be exposed.

But I set out to tell you about Sonny's christenin' an' us turnin' 'Piscopal. Ez I said, he never seemed to want baptism, though he had heard us discuss all his life both it an' vaccination ez the two ordeels to be gone thoo with some time, an' we'd speculate ez to whether vaccination would take or not, an' all sech ez that, an' then, ez I said, after he see what the vaccination was, why he was even mo' prejudyced agin' baptism 'n ever, an' we 'lowed to let it run on tell sech a time ez he'd decide what name he'd want to take an' what denomination he'd want to bestow it on him.

Wife, she's got some 'Piscopal relations thet she sort o' looks up to,—though she don't own it,—but she was raised Methodist an' I was raised a true-blue Presbyterian. But when we professed after Sonny come we went up together at Methodist meetin'. What we was after was righteous livin', an' we didn't keer much which denomination helped us to it.

An' so, feelin' friendly all roun' that-a-way, we thought we'd leave Sonny to pick his church when he got ready, an' then they wouldn't be nothin' to undo or do over in case he went over to the 'Piscopals, which has the name of revisin' over any other church's performances—though sence we've turned 'Piscopals we've found out that ain't so.

Of co'se the preachers, they used to talk to us about it once-t in a while,— seemed to think it ought to be did,—'ceptin', of co'se, the Baptists.

Well, sir, it went along so till last week. Sonny ain't but, ez I said, thess not quite six year old, an' they seemed to be time enough. But last week he had been playin' out o' doors bare-feeted, thess same ez he always does, an' he tramped on a pine splinter some way. Of co'se, pine, it's the safe-t-est splinter a person can run into a foot, on account of its carryin' its own turpentine in with it to heal up things; but any splinter thet dast to push itself up into a little pink foot is a messenger of trouble, an' we know it. An' so, when we see this one, we tried ever' way to coax him to let us take it out, but he wouldn't, of co'se. He never will, an' somehow the Lord seems to give 'em ambition to work their own way out mos' gen'ally.

But, sir, this splinter didn't seem to have no energy in it. It thess lodged there, an' his little foot it commenced to swell, an' it swole an' swole tell his little toes stuck out so thet the little pig thet went to market looked like ez ef it wasn't on speakin' terms with the little pig thet stayed home, an' wife an' me we watched it, an' I reckon she prayed over it consider'ble, an' I read a extry psalm at night befo' I went to bed, all on account o' that little foot. An' night befo' las' it was lookin' mighty angry an' swole, an' he had limped an' "ouched!" consider'ble all day, an' he was mighty fretful bed-time. So, after he went to sleep, wife she come out on the po'ch where I was settin', and she says to me, says she, her face all drawed up an' workin', says she: "Honey," says she, "I reckon we better sen' for him an' have it did." Thess so, she said it. "Sen' for who, wife?" says I, "an' have what did?" "Why, sen' for him, the 'Piscopal preacher," says she, "an' have Sonny christened. Them little toes o' hisn is ez red ez cherry tomatoes. They burnt my lips thess now like a coal o' fire an'—an' lockjaw is goin' roun' tur'ble.

"Seems to me," says she, "when he started to git sleepy, he didn't gap ez wide ez he gen'ly does—an' I'm 'feered he's a-gittin' it now." An', sir, with that, she thess gathered up her apron an' mopped her face in it an' give way. An' ez for me, I didn't seem to have no mo' backbone down my spinal colume 'n a feather bolster has, I was that weak.

I never ast her why she didn't sen' for our own preacher. I knowed then ez well ez ef she'd 'a' told me why she done it—all on account o' Sonny bein' so tickled over the 'Piscopals' meetin's.

It was mos' nine o'clock then, an' a dark night, an' rainin', but I never said a word—they wasn't no room round the edges o' the lump in my throat for words to come out ef they'd 'a' been one surgin' up there to say, which they wasn't— but I thess went out an' saddled my horse an' I rid into town. Stopped first at the doctor's an' sent him out, though I knowed 't wouldn't do no good; Sonny wouldn't 'low him to tech it; but I sent him out anyway, to look at it, an', ef possible, console wife a little. Then I rid on to the rector's an' ast him to come out immejate an' baptize Sonny. But nex' day was his turn to preach down at Sandy Crik, an' he couldn't come that night, but he promised to come right after services nex' mornin'—which he done—rid the whole fo'teen mile from Sandy Crik here in the rain, too, which I think is a evidence o' Christianity, though no sech acts is put down in my book o' "evidences" where they ought rightfully to be.

Well, sir, when I got home that night, I found wife a heap cheerfuler. The doctor had give Sonny a big apple to eat an' pernounced him free from all symptoms o' lockjaw. But when I come the little feller had crawled 'way back under the bed an' lay there, eatin' his apple, an' they couldn't git him out. Soon ez the doctor had teched a poultice to his foot he had woke up an' put a stop to it, an' then he had went off by hisself where nothin' couldn't pester him, to enjoy his apple in peace. An' we never got him out tell he heered us tellin' the doctor good-night.

I tried ever' way to git him out—even took up a coal o' fire an' poked it under at him; but he thess laughed at that an' helt his apple agin' it an' made it sizz. Well, sir, he seemed so tickled thet I helt that coal o' fire for him tell he cooked a good big spot on one side o' the apple, an' et it, an' then, when I took it out, he called for another, but I didn't give it to him. I don't see no use in over-indulgin' a child. An' when he knowed the doctor was gone, he come out an' finished roastin' his apple by the fire—thess what was left of it 'round the co'e.

Well, sir, we was mightily comforted by the doctor's visit, but nex' mornin' things looked purty gloomy ag'in. That little foot seemed a heap worse, an' he was sort o' flushed an' feverish, an' wife she thought she heard a owl hoot, an' Rover made a mighty funny gurgly sound in his th'oat like ez ef he had bad news to tell us, but didn't have the courage to speak it.

An' then, on top o' that, the nigger Dicey, she come in an' 'lowed she had dreamed that night about eatin' spare-ribs, which everybody knows to dream about fresh pork out o' season, which this is July, is considered a shore sign o' death. Of co'se, wife an' me, we don't b'lieve in no sech ez that, but ef you ever come to see yo' little feller's toes stand out the way Sonny's done day befo' yesterday, why, sir, you'll be ready to b'lieve anything. It's so much better now, you can't judge of its looks day befo' yesterday. We never had even so much ez considered it necessary thet little children should be christened to have 'em saved, but when things got on the ticklish edge, like they was then, why, we felt thet the safest side is the wise side, an', of co'se, we want Sonny to have the best of everything. So, we was mighty thankful when we see the rector comin'. But, sir, when I went out to open the gate for him, what on top o' this round hemisp'ere do you reckon Sonny done? Why, sir, he thess took one look at the gate an' then he cut an' run hard ez he could—limped acrost the yard thess like a flash o' zig-zag lightnin'—an' 'fore anybody could stop him, he had clumb to the tip top o' the butter-bean arbor—clumb it thess like a cat—an' there he set, a-swingin' his feet under him, an' laughin', the rain thess a-streakin' his hair all over his face.

That bean arbor is a favoryte place for him to escape to, 'cause it's too high to reach, an' it ain't strong enough to bear no grown-up person's weight.

Well, sir, the rector, he come in an' opened his valise an' 'rayed hisself in his robes an' opened his book, an' while he was turnin' the leaves, he faced 'round an' says he, lookin' at me direc', says he:

"Let the child be brought forward for baptism," says he, thess that-a-way.

Well, sir, I looked at wife, an' wife, she looked at me, an' then we both thess looked out at the butter-bean arbor.

I knowed then thet Sonny wasn't never comin' down while the rector was there, an' rector, he seemed sort o' fretted for a minute when he see how things was, an' he did try to do a little settin' fo'th of opinions. He 'lowed, speakin' in a mighty pompious manner, thet holy things wasn't to be trifled with, an' thet he had come to baptize the child accordin' to the rites o' the church.

'Name this child.'
'Name this child.'
Well, that sort o' talk, it thess rubbed me the wrong way, an' I up an' told him thet that might be so, but thet the rites o' the church didn't count for nothin', on our farm, to the rights o' the boy!

I reckon it was mighty disrespec'ful o' me to face him that-a-way, an' him adorned in all his robes, too, but I'm thess a plain up-an'-down man an' I hadn't went for him to come an' baptize Sonny to uphold the granjer of no church. I was ready to do that when the time come, but right now we was workin' in Sonny's interests, an' I intended to have it understood that way. An' it was.

Rector, he's a mighty good, kind-hearted man, git down to the man inside the preacher, an' when he see thess how things stood, why, he come 'round friendly, an' he went out on the po'ch an' united with us in tryin' to help coax Sonny down. First started by promisin' him speritual benefits, but he soon see that wasn't no go, and he tried worldly persuasion; but no, sir, stid o' him comin' down, Sonny started orderin' the rest of us christened thess the way he done about the vaccination. But, of co'se, we had been baptized befo', an' we nachelly helt out agin' that for some time. But d'rec'ly rector, he seemed to have a sudden idee, an' says he, facin' 'round, church-like, to wife an' me, says he:

"Have you both been baptized accordin' to the rites o' the church?"

An' me, thinkin' of co'se he meant the 'Piscopal Church, says: "No, sir," says I, thess so. And then we see that the way was open for us to be did over ag'in ef we wanted to. So, sir, wife an' me we was took into the church, then an' there. We wouldn't a yielded to him, thoo an' thoo, that-a-way ag'in ef his little foot hadn't a' been so swole, an' he maybe takin' his death o' cold settin' out in the po'in'-down rain; but things bein' as they was, we went thoo it with all due respects.

Then he commenced callin' for Dicey, an' the dog, an' the cat, to be did, same ez he done befo'; but, of co'se, they's some liberties thet even a innocent child can't take with the waters o' baptism, an' the rector he got sort o' wo'e-out and disgusted an' 'lowed thet 'less'n we could get the child ready for baptism he'd haf to go home.

Well, sir, I knowed we wouldn't never git 'im down, an' I had went for the rector to baptize him, an' I intended to have it did, ef possible. So, says I, turnin' 'round an' facin' him square, says I: "Rector," says I, "why not baptize him where he is? I mean it. The waters o' Heaven are descendin' upon him where he sets, an' seems to me ef he's favo'bly situated for anything it is for baptism." Well, parson, he thess looked at me up an' down for a minute, like ez ef he s'picioned I was wanderin' in my mind, but he didn't faze me. I thess kep' up my argiment. Says I: "Parson," says I, speakin' thess ez ca'm ez I am this minute—"Parson," says I, "his little foot is mighty swole, an' so'e, an' that splinter—thess s'pose he was to take the lockjaw an' die—don't you reckon you might do it where he sets—from where you stand?"

Wife, she was cryin' by this time, an' parson, he claired his th'oat an' coughed, an' then he commenced walkin' up an' down, an' treckly he stopped, an' says he, speakin' mighty reverential an' serious:

"Lookin' at this case speritually, an' as a minister o' the Gospel," says he, "it seems to me thet the question ain't so much a question of doin' ez it is a question of withholdin'. I don't know," says he, "ez I've got a right to withhold the sacrament o' baptism from a child under these circumstances or to deny sech comfort to his parents ez lies in my power to bestow."

An', sir, with that he stepped out to the end o' the po'ch, opened his book ag'in, an' holdin' up his right hand to'ards Sonny, settin' on top o' the bean-arbor in the rain, he commenced to read the service o' baptism, an' we stood proxies—which is a sort o' a dummy substitutes—for whatever godfather an' mother Sonny see fit to choose in after life.

Parson, he looked half like ez ef he'd laugh once-t. When he had thess opened his book and started to speak, a sudden streak o' sunshine shot out an' the rain started to ease up, an' it looked for a minute ez ef he was goin' to lose the baptismal waters. But d'rec'ly it come down stiddy ag'in an he' went thoo the programme entire.

An' Sonny, he behaved mighty purty; set up perfec'ly ca'm an' composed thoo it all, an' took everything in good part, though he didn't p'intedly know who was bein' baptized, 'cause, of co'se, he couldn't hear the words with the rain in his ears.

He didn't rightly sense the situation tell it come to the part where it says: "Name this child," and, of co'se, I called out to Sonny to name hisself, which it had always been our intention to let him do.

"Name yo'self, right quick, like a good boy," says I.

Of co'se Sonny had all his life heered me say thet I was Deuteronomy Jones, Senior, an' thet I hoped some day when he got christened he'd be the junior. He knowed that by heart, an' would agree to it or dispute it, 'cordin' to how the notion took him, and I sort o' ca'culated thet he'd out with it now. But no, sir! Not a word! He thess sot up on thet bean-arbor an' grinned.

An' so, feelin' put to it, with the services suspended over my head, I spoke up, an' I says: "Parson," says I, "I reckon ef he was to speak his little heart, he'd say Deuteronomy Jones, Junior." An' with thet what does Sonny do but conterdic' me flat! "No, not Junior! I want to be named Deuteronomy Jones, Senior!" says he, thess so. An' parson, he looked to'ards me, an' I bowed my head an' he pernouneed thess one single name, "Deuteronomy," an' I see he wasn't goin' to say no more an' so I spoke up quick, an' says I: "Parson," says I, "he has spoke his heart's desire. He has named hisself after me entire—Deuteronomy Jones, Senior."

An' so he was obligated to say it, an' so it is writ in the family record colume in the big Bible, though I spelt his Senior with a little s, an' writ him down ez the only son of the Senior with the big S, which it seems to me fixes it about right for the time bein'.

'An' then Sonny, seein' it all over, he come down.'
'An' then Sonny, seein' it all over, he come down.'
Well, when the rector had got thoo an' he had wropped up his robes an' put 'em in his wallet, an' had told us to prepare for conformation, he pernounced a blessin' upon us an' went.

Then Sonny seein' it was all over, why, he come down. He was wet ez a drownded rat, but wife rubbed him off an' give him some hot tea an' he come a-snuggin' up in my lap, thess ez sweet a child ez you ever see in yo' life, an' I talked to him ez fatherly ez I could, told him we was all 'Piscopals now, an' soon ez his little foot got well I was goin' to take him out to Sunday-school to tote a banner—all his little 'Piscopal friends totes banners—an' thet he could pick out some purty candles for the altar, an' he 'lowed immejate thet he'd buy pink ones. Sonny always was death on pink—showed it from the time he could snatch a pink rose—an' wife she ain't never dressed him in nothin' else. Ever' pair o' little breeches he's got is either pink or pink-trimmed.

Well, I talked along to him till I worked 'round to shamin' him a little for havin' to be christened settin' up on top a bean-arbor, same ez a crow-bird, which I told him the parson he wouldn't 'a' done ef he 'd 'a' felt free to 've left it undone. 'Twasn't to indulge him he done it, but to bless him an' to comfort our hearts. Well, after I had reasoned with him severe that-a-way a while, he says, says he, thess ez sweet an' mild, says he, "Daddy, nex' time y'all gits christened, I'll come down an' be elms-tened right—like a good boy."

Th' ain't a sweeter child in'ardly 'n what Sonny is, nowheres, git him to feel right comf'table, an' I know it, an' that's why I have patience with his little out'ard ways.

"Yes, sir," says he; "nex' time I 'll be christened like a good boy."

Then, of co'se, I explained to him thet it couldn't never be did no mo', 'cause it had been did, an' did 'Piscopal, which is secure. An' then what you reckon the little feller said?

Says he, "Yes, daddy, but s'pos'in' mine don't take. How 'bout that?"

An' I didn't try to explain no further. What was the use? Wife, she had drawed a stool close-t up to my knee, an' set there sortin' out the little yaller rings ez they 'd dry out on his head, an' when he said that I thess looked at her an' we both looked at him, an' says I, "Wife," says I, "ef they's anything in heavenly looks an' behavior, I b'lieve that christenin' is started to take on him a'ready."

An' I b'lieve it had.

SONNY'S SCHOOLIN'

Well, sir, we're tryin' to edjercate him—good ez we can. Th' ain't never been a edjercational advantage come in reach of us but we've give it to him. Of co'se he's all we've got, that one boy is, an' wife an' me, why, we feel the same way about it.

They's three schools in the county, not countin' the niggers', an' we send him to all three.

Sir? Oh, yas, sir; he b'longs to all three schools—to fo' for that matter, countin' the home school.

You see, Sonny he's purty ticklish to handle, an' a person has to know thess how to tackle him. Even wife an' me, thet's been knowin' him f'om the beginnin', not only knowin' his traits, but how he come by 'em,—though some is hard to trace to their so'ces,—why, sir, even we have to study sometimes to keep in with him, an' of co'se a teacher—why, it's thess hit an' miss whether he'll take the right tack with him or not; an' sometimes one teacher'll strike it one day, an' another nex' day; so by payin' schoolin' for him right along in all three, why, of co'se, ef he don't feel like goin' to one, why, he'll go to another.

Once-t in a while he'll git out with the whole of 'em, an' that was how wife come to open the home school for him. She was determined his edjercation shouldn't be interrupted ef she could help it. She don't encour'ge him much to go to her school, though, 'cause it interrupts her in her housekeepin' consider'ble, an' she's had extry quilt-patchin' on hand ever since he come. She's patchin' him a set 'ginst the time he'll marry.

'An' then I reckon he frets her a good deal in school. Somehow, seems like he thess picks up enough in the other schools to be able to conterdic' her ways o' teachin'.

F' instance, in addin' up a colume o' figgers, ef she comes to a aught—which some calls 'em naughts—she'll say, "Aught's a aught," an' Sonny ain't been learned to say it that a-way; an' so maybe when she says, "Aught's a aught," he'll say, "Who said it wasn't!" an' that puts her out in countin'.

He's been learned to thess pass over aughts an' not call their names; and once-t or twice-t, when wife called 'em out that a-way, why, he got so fretted he thess gethered up his things an' went to another school. But seem like she's added aughts that a-way so long she can't think to add 'em no other way.

I notice nights after she's kept school for Sonny all day she talks consider'ble in her sleep, an' she says, "Aught's a aught" about ez often ez she says anything else.

Oh, yas, sir; he's had consider'ble fusses with his teachers, one way an' another, but they ever'one declare they think a heap of 'im.

Sir? Oh, yas, sir; of co'se they all draw their reg'lar pay whether he's a day in school du'in' the month or not. That's right enough, 'cause you see they don't know what day he's li'ble to drop in on 'em, an' it's worth the money thess a-keepin' their nerves strung for 'im.

Well, yas, sir; 't is toler'ble expensive, lookin' at it one way, but lookin' at it another, it don't cost no mo' 'n what it would to edjercate three child'en, which many poor families have to do—an' more—which in our united mind Sonny's worth 'em all.

Yas, sir; 't is confusin' to him in some ways, goin' to all three schools at once-t.

F' instance, Miss Alviry Sawyer, which she's a single-handed maiden lady 'bout wife's age, why, of co'se, she teaches accordin' to the old rules; an' in learnin' the child'en subtraction, f' instance, she'll tell 'em, ef they run short to borry one fom the nex' lef' han' top figur', an' pay it back to the feller underneath him.

Well, this didn't suit Sonny's sense o' jestice no way, borryin' from one an' payin' back to somebody else; so he thess up an argued about it—told her thet fellers thet borried nickels fom one another couldn't pay back that a-way; an' of co'se she told him they was heap o' difference 'twix' money and 'rithmetic—which I wish't they was more in my experience; an' so they had it hot and heavy for a while, till at last she explained to him thet that way of doin' subtraction fetched the answer, which, of co'se, ought to satisfy any school-boy; an' I reckon Sonny would soon 'a' settled into that way 'ceptin' thet he got out o' patience with that school in sev'al ways, an' he left an' went out to Sandy Crik school, and it thess happened that he struck a subtraction class there the day he got in, an' they was workin' it the other way—borry one from the top figur' an' never pay it back at all, thess count it off (that's the way I 've worked my lifelong subtraction, though wife does hers payin' back), an' of co'se Sonny was ready to dispute this way, an' he didn't have no mo' tac' than to th'ow up Miss Alviry's way to the teacher, which of co'se he wouldn't stand, particular ez Miss Alviry's got the biggest school. So they broke up in a row, immejate, and Sonny went right along to Miss Kellogg's school down here at the cross-roads.

She's a sort o' reformed teacher, I take it; an' she gets at her subtraction by a new route altogether—like ez ef the first feller thet had any surplus went sort o security for them thet was short, an' passed the loan down the line. But I noticed he never got his money back, for when they come to him, why, they docked him. I reckon goin' security is purty much the same in an out o' books. She passes the borryin' along some way till it gits to headquarters, an' writes a new row o' figur's over the heads o' the others. Well, my old brain got so addled watchin' Sonny work it thet I didn't seem to know one figur' fom another 'fo' he got thoo; but when I see the answer come, why, I was satisfied. Ef a man can thess git his answers right all his life, why nobody ain't a-goin' to pester him about how he worked his figur's.

I did try to get Sonny to stick to one school for each rule in 'rithmetic, an' havin' thess fo' schools, why he could learn each o' the fo' rules by one settled plan. But he wont promise nothin'. He'll quit for lessons one week, and maybe next week somethin' else 'll decide him. (He's quit ever' one of 'em in turn when they come to long division.) He went thoo a whole week o' disagreeable lessons once-t at one school 'cause he was watchin' a bird-nest on the way to that school. He was determined them young birds was to be allowed to leave that nest without bein' pestered, an' they stayed so long they purty nigh run him into long division 'fo' they did fly. Ef he'd 'a' missed school one day he knowed two sneaky chaps thet would 'a' robbed that nest, either goin' or comin'.

Of co'se Sonny goes to the exhibitions an' picnics of all the schools. Last summer we had a time of it when it come picnic season. Two schools set the same day for theirs, which of co'se wasn't no ways fair to Sonny. He payin' right along in all the schools, of co'se he was entitled to all the picnics; so I put on my Sunday clo'es, an' I went down an' had it fixed right. They all wanted Sonny, too, come down to the truth, 'cause besides bein' fond of him, they knowed thet Sonny always fetched a big basket.

'He was watchin' a bird-nest on the way to that school.'
'He was watchin' a bird-nest on the way to that school.'
Trouble with Sonny is thet he don't take nothin' on nobody's say-so, don't keer who it is. He even commenced to dispute Moses one Sunday when wife was readin' the Holy Scriptures to him, tell of co'se she made him understand thet that wouldn't do. Moses didn't intend to be conterdicted.

An' ez to secular lessons, he ain't got no espec' for 'em whatsoever. F' instance, when the teacher learned him thet the world was round, why he up an' told him 't warn't so, less'n we was on the inside an' it was blue-lined, which of co'se teacher he insisted thet we was on the outside, walkin' over it, all feet todes the center—a thing I've always thought myself was mo' easy said than proved.

Well, sir, Sonny didn't hesitate to deny it, an' of co'se teacher he commenced by givin' him a check—which is a bad mark—for conterdictin'. An' then Sonny he 'lowed thet he didn't conterdic' to be aconterdictin', but he knowed't warn't so. He had walked the whole len'th o' the road 'twix' the farm an' the school-house, an' they warn't no bulge in it; an' besides, he hadn't never saw over the edges of it.

An' with that teacher he give him another check for speakin' out o' turn. An' then Sonny, says he, "Ef a man was tall enough he could see around the edges, couldn't he?" "No," says the teacher; "a man couldn't grow that tall," says he; "he'd be deformed."

An' Sonny, why, he spoke up again, an' says he, "But I'm thess a-sayin' ef," says he. "An' teacher," says he, "we ain't a-studyin' efs; we're studyin' geoger'phy." And then Sonny they say he kep' still a minute, an' then he says, says he, "Oh, maybe he couldn't see over the edges, teacher, 'cause ef he was tall enough his head might reach up into the flo' o' heaven." And with that teacher he give him another check, an' told him not to dare to mix up geoger'phy an' religion, which was a sackerlege to both studies; an' with that Sonny gethered up his books an' set out to another school.

I think myself it 'u'd be thess ez well ef Sonny wasn't quite so quick to conterdic'; but it's thess his way of holdin' his p'int.

Why, one day he faced one o' the teachers down thet two an' two didn't haf to make fo', wh'er or no.

This seemed to tickle the teacher mightily, an' so he laughed an' told him he was goin' to give him rope enough to hang hisself now, an' then he dared him to show him any two an' two thet didn't make fo', and Sonny says, says he, "Heap o' two an' twos don't make four, 'cause they're kep' sep'rate," says he.

"An' then," says he, "I don't want my two billy-goats harnessed up with nobody else's two billys to make fo' billys."

"But," says the teacher, "suppose I was to harness up yo' two goats with Tom Deems's two, there'd be fo' goats, I reckon, whether you wanted 'em there or not."

"No they wouldn't," says Sonny. "They wouldn't be but two. 'T wouldn't take my team more 'n half a minute to butt the life out o' Tom's team."

An' with that little Tommy Deems, why, he commenced to cry, an' 'stid o' punishin' him for bein' sech a cry-baby, what did the teacher do but give Sonny another check, for castin' slurs on Tommy's animals, an' gettin' Tommy's feelin's hurted! Which I ain't a-sayin' it on account o' Sonny bein' my boy, but it seems to me was a mighty unfair advantage.

No boy's feelin's ain't got no right to be that tender—an' a goat is the last thing on earth thet could be injured by a word of mouth.

Sonny's pets an' beasts has made a heap o' commotion in school one way an' another, somehow. Ef 't ain't his goats it's somethin' else.

Sir! Sonny's pets? Oh, they're all sorts. He ain't no ways partic'lar thess so a thing is po' an' miser'ble enough. That's about all he seems to require of anything.

He don't never go to school hardly 'thout a garter-snake or two or a lizard or a toad-frog somewheres about him. He's got some o' the little girls at school that nervous thet if he thess shakes his little sleeve at 'em they'll squeal, not knowin' what sort o' live critter'll jump out of it.

Most of his pets is things he's got by their bein' hurted some way.

One of his toad-frogs is blind of a eye. Sonny rescued him from the old red rooster one day after he had nearly pecked him to death, an' he had him hoppin' round the kitchen for about a week with one eye bandaged up.

When a hurted critter gits good an' strong he gen'ally turns it loose ag'in; but ef it stays puny, why he reg'lar 'dopts it an' names it Jones. That's thess a little notion o' his, namin' his pets the family name.

The most outlandish thing he ever 'dopted, to my mind, is that old yaller cat. That was a miser'ble low-down stray cat thet hung round the place a whole season, an' Sonny used to vow he was goin' to kill it, 'cause it kep' a-ketchin' the birds.

Well, one day he happened to see him thess runnin' off with a young mockin'-bird in his mouth, an' he took a brickbat an' he let him have it, an' of co'se he dropped the bird an' tumbled over—stunted. The bird it got well, and Sonny turned him loose after a few days; but that cat was hurted fatal. He couldn't never no mo' 'n drag hisself around from that day to this; an' I reckon ef Sonny was called on to give up every pet he's got, that cat would be 'bout the last thing he'd surrender. He named him Tommy Jones, an' he never goes to school of a mornin', rain or shine, till Tommy Jones is fed f'om his own plate with somethin' he's left for him special.

Of co'se Sonny he's got his faults, which anybody 'll tell you; but th' ain't a dumb brute on the farm but'll foller him around—an' the nigger Dicey, why, she thinks they never was such another boy born into the world—that is, not no human child.

An' wife an' me—

But of co'se he's ours.

I don't doubt thet he ain't constructed thess exac'ly ez the school-teachers would have him, ef they had their way. Sometimes I have thought I'd like his disposition eased up a little, myself, when he taken a stand ag'in my judgment or wife's.

Takin' 'em all round, though, the teachers has been mighty patient with him.

At one school the teacher did take him out behind the school-house one day to whup him; an' although teacher is a big strong man, Sonny's mighty wiry an' quick, an' some way he slipped his holt, an' fo' teacher could ketch him ag'in he had clumb up the lightnin'-rod on to the roof thess like a cat. An' teacher he felt purty shore of him then, 'cause he 'lowed they wasn't no other way to git down (which they wasn't, the school bein' a steep-sided buildin'), an' he 'd wait for him.

So teacher he set down close-t to the lightnin'-rod to wait. He wouldn't go back in school without him, cause he didn't want the child'en to know he'd got away. So down he set; but he hadn't no mo' 'n took his seat sca'cely when he heerd the child'en in school roa'in' out loud, laughin' fit to kill theirselves.

He lowed at first thet like ez not the monitor was cuttin' up some sort o' didoes, the way monitors does gen'ally, so he waited a-while; but it kep' a-gittin' worse, so d'rectly he got up, an' he went in to see what the excitement was about; an'lo and beholt! Sonny had slipped down the open chimbly right in amongst 'em—come out a-grinnin', with his face all sooted over, an', says he, "Say, fellers," says he, "I run up the lightnin'-rod, an' he's a-waitin' for me to come down." An' with that he went an' gethered up his books, deliberate, an'fetched his hat, an' picked up a nest o' little chimbly-swallows he had dislodged in comin' down (all this here it happened thess las' June), an' he went out an' harnessed up his goat-wagon, an' got in. An' thess ez he driv' out the school-yard into the road the teacher come in, an' he see how things was.

Of co'se sech conduct ez that is worrisome, but I don't see no, to say, bad principle in it. Sonny ain't got a bad habit on earth, not a-one. They'll ever' one o' the teachers tell you that. He ain't never been knowed to lie, an' ez for improper language, why he wouldn't know how to select it. An' ez to tattlin' at home about what goes on in school, why, he never has did it. The only way we knowed about him comin' down the school-house chimbly was wife went to fetch his dinner to him, an' she found it out.

 'He had been playin' out o' doors bare-feeted.'
'He had been playin' out o' doors bare-feeted.'
She knowed he had went to that school in the mornin', an' when she got there at twelve o'clock, why he wasn't there, an' of co'se she questioned the teacher, an' he thess told her thet Sonny had been present at the mornin' session, but thet he was now absent. An' the rest of it she picked out o' the child'en.

Oh, no, sir; she don't take his dinner to him reg'lar—only some days when she happens to have somethin' extry good, or maybe when she 'magines he didn't eat hearty at breakfast. The school-child'en they always likes to see her come, because she gen'ally takes a extry lot o' fried chicken thess for him to give away. He don't keer much for nothin' but livers an' gizzards, so we have to kill a good many to get enough for him; an' of co'se the fryin' o' the rest of it is mighty little trouble.

Sonny is a bothersome child one way: he don't never want to take his dinner to school with him. Of co'se thess after eatin' breakfas' he don't feel hungry, an' when wife does coax him to take it, he'll seem to git up a appetite walkin' to school, an' he'll eat it up 'fo' he gits there.

Sonny's got a mighty noble disposition, though, take him all round.

Now, the day he slipped down that chimbly an' run away he wasn't a bit flustered, an' he didn't play hookey the balance of the day neither. He thess went down to the crik, an' washed the soot off his face, though they say he didn't no more 'n smear it round, an' then he went down to Miss Phoebe's school, an' stayed there till it was out. An' she took him out to the well, an' washed his face good for him. But nex' day he up an' went back to Mr. Clark's school—walked in thess ez pleasant an' kind, an' taken his seat an' said his lessons—never th'owed it up to teacher at all. Now, some child'en, after playin' off on a teacher that a-way would a' took advantage, but he never. It was a fair fight, an' Sonny whupped, an' that's all there was to it; an' he never put on no air about it.

Wife did threaten to go herself an' make the teacher apologize for gittin' the little feller all sooted up an' sp'iln' his clo'es; but she thought it over, an' she decided thet she wouldn't disturb things ez long ez they was peaceful. An', after all, he didn't exac'ly send him down the chimbly nohow, though he provoked him to it.

Ef Sonny had 'a' fell an' hurted hisself, though, in that chimbly, I'd 'a' helt that teacher responsible, shore.

Sonny says hisself thet the only thing he feels bad about in that chimbly business is thet one o' the little swallers' wings was broke by the fall. Sonny's got him yet, an' he's li'ble to keep him, cause he'll never fly. Named him Swally Jones, an' reg'lar 'dopted him soon ez he see how his wing was.

Sonny's the only child I ever see in my life thet could take young chimbly-swallers after their fall an' make em' live. But he does it reg'lar. They ain't a week passes sca'cely but he fetches in some hurted critter an' works with it. Dicey says thet half the time she's afeerd to step around her cook-stove less'n she'll step on some critter thet's crawled back to life where he's put it under the stove to hatch or thaw out, which she bein' bare-feeted, I don't wonder at.

An' he has did the same way at school purty much. It got so for a-while at one school thet not a child in school could be hired to put his hand in the wood-box, not knowin' ef any piece o' bark or old wood in it would turn out to be a young alligator or toad-frog thawin' out. Teacher hisself picked up a chip, reckless, one day, an' it hopped up, and knocked off his spectacles. Of cose it wasn't no chip. Hopper-toad frogs an' wood-bark chips, why, they favors consider'ble—lay 'em same side up.

It was on account o' her takin' a interest in all his little beasts an' varmints thet he first took sech a notion to Miss Phoebe Kellog's school. Where any other teacher would scold about sech things ez he'd fetch in, why, she'd encourage him to bring 'em to her; an' she'd fix a place for 'em, an' maybe git out some book tellin' all about 'em, an' showin' pictures of 'em.

She's had squir'l-books, an' bird-books, an' books on nearly every sort o' wild critter you'd think too mean to put into a book, at that school, an' give the child'en readin'-lessons on 'em an' drawin'-lessons an' clay-moldin' lessons.

Why, Sonny has did his alligator so nach'l in clay thet you'd most expec' to see it creep away. An' you'd think mo' of alligators forever afterward, too. An' ez to readin', he never did take no interest in learnin' how to read out'n them school-readers, which he declares don't no more'n git a person interested in one thing befo' they start on another, an' maybe start that in the middle.

The other teachers, they makes a heap o' fun o' Miss Phoebe's way o' school-teachin', 'cause she lets the child'en ask all sorts of outlandish questions, an' make pictures in school hours, an' she don't requi' 'em to fold their arms in school, neither.

Maybe she is foolin' their time away. I can't say ez I exac'ly see how she's a workin' it to edjercate 'em that a-way. I had to set with my arms folded eight hours a day in school when I was a boy, to learn the little I know, an' wife she got her edjercation the same way. An' we went clean thoo f'om the a-b abs an' e-b ebs clair to the end o' the blue-back speller.

An' we learned to purnounce a heap mo' words than either one of us has ever needed to know, though there has been times, sech ez when my wife's mother took the phthisic an' I had the asthma, thet I was obligated to write to the doctor about it, thet I was thankful for my experience in the blue-back speller. Them was our brag-words, phthisic and asthma was. They's a few other words I've always hoped to have a chance to spell in the reg'lar co'se of life, sech ez y-a-c-h-t, yacht, but I suppose, livin' in a little inland town, which a yacht is a boat, a person couldn't be expected to need sech a word—less'n he went travelin'.

I've often thought thet ef at the Jedgment the good Lord would only examine me an' all them thet went to school in my day, in the old blue-back speller 'stid o' tacklin' us on the weak pints of our pore mortal lives, why, we'd stand about ez good a chance o' gettin' to heaven ez anybody else. An' maybe He will—who knows?

But ez for book-readin', wife an' me aint never felt called on to read no book save an' exceptin' the Holy Scriptures—an', of cose, the seed catalogues.

An' here Sonny, not quite twelve year old, has read five books thoo, an' some of 'em twice-t an' three times over. His "Robinson Crusoe" shows mo' wear'n tear'n what my Testament does, I'm ashamed to say. I've done give Miss Phoebe free license to buy him any book she wants him to have, an' he's got 'em all 'ranged in a row on the end o' the mantel-shelf.

Quick ez he'd git thoo readin' a book, of co'se wife she'd be for dustin' it off and puttin' up on the top closet shelf where a book nach'ally belongs; but seem like Sonny he wants to keep 'em in sight. So wife she'd worked a little lace shelf-cover to lay under 'em, an' we've hung our framed marriage-c'tificate above 'em, an' the corner looks right purty, come to see it fixed up.

Sir? Oh, no; we ain't took him from none o' the other schools yet. He's been goin' to Miss Phoebe's reg'lar now—all but the exhibition an' picnic days in the other schools—for nearly five months, not countin' off-an'-on days he went to her befo' he settled down to it stiddy.

He says he's a-goin' there reg'lar from this time on, an' I b'lieve he will; but wife an' me we talked it over, an' we decided we'd let things stand, an' keep his name down on all the books till sech a time ez he come to long division with Miss Kellog.

An' ef he stays thoo that, we'll feel free to notify the other schools thet he's quit.

SONNY'S DIPLOMA

Yas, sir; this is it. This here's Sonny's diplomy thet you've heerd so much about—sheepskin they call it, though it ain't no mo' sheepskin 'n what I am. I've skinned too many not to know. Thess to think o' little Sonny bein' a grad'jate—an' all by his own efforts, too! It is a plain-lookin' picture, ez you say, to be framed up in sech a fine gilt frame; but it's worth it, an' I don't begrudge it to him. He picked out that red plush hisself. He's got mighty fine taste for a country-raised child, Sonny has.

Seem like the oftener I come here an' stan' before it, the prouder I feel, an' the mo' I can't reelize thet he done it.

I'd 'a' been proud enough to've had him go through the reg'lar co'se o' study, an' be awarded this diplomy, but to 've seen 'im thess walk in an' demand it, the way he done, an' to prove his right in a fair fight—why, it tickles me so thet I thess seem to git a spell o' the giggles ev'y time I think about it.

Sir? How did he do it? Why, I thought eve'ybody in the State of Arkansas knowed how Sonny walked over the boa'd o' school directors, an' took a diplomy in the face of Providence, at the last anniversary.

I don't know thet I ought to say that either, for they never was a thing done mo' friendly an' amiable on earth, on his part, than the takin' of this dockiment. Why, no; of co'se he wasn't goin' to that school—cert'n'y not. Ef he had b'longed to that school, they wouldn't 'a' been no question about it. He 'd 'a' thess gradj'ated with the others. An' when he went there with his ma an' me, why, he'll tell you hisself that he hadn't no mo' idee of gradj'atin' 'n what I have this minute.

An' when he riz up in his seat, an' announced his intention, why, you could 'a' knocked me down with a feather. You see, it took me so sudden, an' I didn't see thess how he was goin' to work it, never havin' been to that school.

Of co'se eve'ybody in the county goes to the gradj'atin', an' we was all three settin' there watchin' the performances, not thinkin' of any special excitement, when Sonny took this idee.

It seems thet seein' all the other boys gradj'ate put him in the notion, an' he felt like ez ef he ought to be a-gradj'atin', too.

You see, he had went to school mo' or less with all them fellers, an' he knowed thet they didn't, none o' 'em, know half ez much ez what he did,—though, to tell the truth, he ain't never said sech a word, not even to her or me,—an', seein' how easy they was bein' turned out, why, he thess reelized his own rights—an' demanded 'em then an' there.

Of co'se we know thet they is folks in this here community thet says thet he ain't got no right to this dipiomy; but what else could you expect in a jealous neighborhood where eve'ybody is mo' or less kin?

The way I look at it, they never was a diplomy earned quite so upright ez this on earth—never. Ef it wasn't, why, I wouldn't allow him to have it, no matter how much pride I would 'a' took, an' do take, in it. But for a boy o' Sonny's age to've had the courage to face all them people, an' ask to be examined then an' there, an' to come out ahead, the way he done, why, it does me proud, that it does.

You see, for a boy to set there seein' all them know-nothin' boys gradj'ate, one after another, offhand, the way they was doin', was mighty provokin', an' when Sonny is struck with a sense of injestice, why, he ain't never been known to bear it in silence. He taken that from her side o' the house.

I noticed, ez he set there that day, thet he begin to look toler'ble solemn, for a festival, but it never crossed my mind what he was a-projeckin' to do. Ef I had 'a' suspicioned it, I'm afeered I would've opposed it, I'd 'a' been so skeert he wouldn't come out all right; an' ez I said, I didn't see, for the life o' me, how he was goin' to work it.

That is the only school in the county thet he ain't never went to, 'cause it was started after he had settled down to Miss Phoebe's school. He wouldn't hardly 'v went to it, nohow, though—less'n, of co'se, he 'd 'a' took a notion. Th' ain't no 'casion to send him to a county school when he's the only one we've got to edjercate. They ain't been a thing I've enjoyed ez much in my life ez my sackerfices on account o' Sonny's edjercation—not a one. Th' ain't a patch on any ol' coat I've got but seems to me to stand for some advantage to him.

Well, sir, it was thess like I'm a-tellin' you. He set still ez long ez he could, an' then he riz an' spoke. Says he, "I have decided thet I'd like to do a little gradj'atin' this evenin' myself," thess that a-way.

An' when he spoke them words, for about a minute you could 'a' heerd a pin drop; an' then eve'ybody begin a-screechin' with laughter. A person would think thet they'd 'a' had some consideration for a child standin' up in the midst o' sech a getherin', tryin' to take his own part; but they didn't. They thess laughed immod'rate. But they didn't faze him. He had took his station on the flo', an' he helt his ground.

Thess ez soon ez he could git a heerin', why, he says, says he: "I don't want anybody to think thet I'm a-tryin' to take any advantage. I don't expec' to gradj'ate without passin' my examination. An', mo' 'n that," says he, "I am ready to pass it now." An' then he went on to explain thet he would like to have anybody present thet was competent to do it to step forward an' examine him— then an' there. An' he said thet ef he was examined fair and square, to the satisfaction of eve'ybody—an' didn't pass—why, he 'd give up the p'int. An' he wanted to be examined oral—in eve'ybody's hearin'—free-handed an' outspoke.

 'Any question he missed was to be passed on to them thet had been grad'jatin' so fast.'
'Any question he missed was to be passed on to them thet had been grad'jatin' so fast.'
Well, sir, seem like folks begin to see a little fun ahead in lettin' him try it— which I don't see thess how they could 'a' hindered him, an' it a free school, an' me a taxpayer. But they all seemed to be in a pretty good humor by this time, an' when Sonny put it to vote, why, they voted unanymous to let him try it. An' all o' them unanymous votes wasn't, to say, friendly, neither. Heap o' them thet was loudest in their unanimosity was hopefully expectin' to see him whipped out at the first question. Tell the truth, I mo' 'n half feared to see it myself. I was that skeert I was fairly all of a trimble.

Well, when they had done votin', Sonny, after first thankin' 'em,—which I think was a mighty polite thing to do, an' they full o' the giggles at his little expense that minute,—why, he went on to say thet he requie'd 'em to make thess one condition, an' that was thet any question he missed was to be passed on to them thet had been a-gradj'atin' so fast, an' ef they missed it, it wasn't to be counted ag'inst him.

Well, when he come out with that, which, to my mind, couldn't be beat for fairness, why, some o' the mothers they commenced to look purty serious, an' seem like ez ef they didn't find it quite so funny ez it had been. You see, they say thet them boys had eve'y one had reg'lar questions give' out to 'em, an' eve'y last one had studied his own word; an' ef they was to be questioned hit an' miss, why they wouldn't 'a' stood no chance on earth.

Of co'se they couldn't give Sonny the same questions thet had been give' out, because he had heerd the answers, an' it wouldn't 'a' been fair. So Sonny he told 'em to thess set down, an' make out a list of questions thet they'd all agree was about of a' equal hardness to them thet had been ast, an' was of thess the kind of learnin' thet all the reg'lar gradj'ates's minds was sto'ed with, an' thet either he knowed 'em or he didn't—one.

It don't seem so excitin', somehow, when I tell about it now; but I tell you for about a minute or so, whilst they was waitin' to see who would undertake the job of examinin' him, why, it seemed thet eve'y minute would be the next, ez my ol' daddy used to say. The only person present thet seemed to take things anyway ca'm was Miss Phoebe Kellog, Sonny's teacher. She has been teachin' him reg'lar for over two years now, an' ef she had 'a' had a right to give diplomies, why, Sonny would 'a' thess took out one from her; but she ain't got no license to gradj'ate nobody. But she knowed what Sonny knowed, an' she knowed thet ef he had a fair show, he'd come thoo creditable to all hands. She loves Sonny thess about ez much ez we do, I believe, take it all round. Th' ain't never been but one time in these two years thet she has, to say, got me out o' temper, an' that was the day she said to me thet her sure belief was thet Sonny was goin' to make somethin' out'n hisself some day—like ez ef he hadn't already made mo' 'n could be expected of a boy of his age. Tell the truth, I never in my life come so near sayin' somethin' I'd 'a' been shore to regret ez I did on that occasion. But of co'se I know she didn't mean it. All she meant was thet he would turn out even mo' 'n what he was now, which would be on'y nachel, with his growth.

Everybody knows thet it was her that got him started with his collections an' his libr'y. Oh, yes; he's got the best libr'y in the county, 'cep'n', of co'se, the doctor's 'n the preacher's—everybody round about here knows about that. He's got about a hund'ed books an' over. Well, sir, when he made that remark, thet any question thet he missed was to be give to the class, why, the whole atmosp'ere took on a change o' temp'ature. Even the teacher was for backin' out o' the whole business square; but he didn't thess seem to dare to say so. You see, after him a-favorin' it, it would 'a' been a dead give-away.

Eve'ybody there had saw him step over an' whisper to Brother Binney when it was decided to give Sonny a chance, an' they knowed thet he had asked him to examine him. But now, instid o' callin' on Brother Binney, why, he thess said, says he: "I suppose I ought not to shirk this duty. Ef it's to be did," says he, "I reckon I ought to do it—an' do it I will." You see, he daresn't allow Brother Binney to put questions, for fear he'd call out some thet his smarty grad'jates couldn't answer.

So he thess claired his th'oat, an' set down a minute to consider. An' then he riz from his seat, an' remarked, with a heap o' hems and haws, thet of co'se everybody knowed thet Sonny Jones had had unusual advantages in some respec's, but thet it was one thing for a boy to spend his time a-picnickin' in the woods, getherin' all sorts of natural curiosities, but it was quite another to be a scholar accordin' to books, so's to be able to pass sech a' examination ez would be a credit to a State institution o' learnin', sech ez the one over which he was proud to preside. That word struck me partic'lar, "proud to preside," which, in all this, of co'se, I see he was castin' a slur on Sonny's collections of birds' eggs, an' his wild flowers, an' wood specimens, an' min'rals. He even went so far ez to say thet ol' Proph', the half-crazy nigger thet tells fortunes, an' gethers herbs out 'n the woods, an' talks to hisself, likely knew more about a good many things than anybody present, but thet, bein' ez he didn't know b from a bull's foot, why, it wouldn't hardly do to grad'jate him—not castin' no slurs on Master Sonny Jones, nor makin' no invijus comparisons, of co'se.

Well, sir, there was some folks there thet seemed to think this sort o' talk was mighty funny an' smart. Some o' the mothers acchilly giggled over it out loud, they was so mightily tickled. But Sonny he thess stood his ground an' waited. Most any boy o' his age would 'a' got flustered, but he didn't. He thess glanced around unconcerned at all the people a-settin' around him, thess like ez ef they might 'a' been askin' him to a picnic instid o' him provokin' a whole school committee to wrath.

Well, sir, it took that school-teacher about a half-hour to pick out the first question, an' he didn't pick it out then. He 'd stop, an' he'd look at the book, an' then he'd look at Sonny, an' then he'd look at the class,—an' then he'd turn a page, like ez ef he couldn't make up his mind, an' was afeerd to resk it, less'n it might be missed, an' be referred back to the class. I never did see a man so overwrought over a little thing in my life—never. They do say, though, that school-teachers feels mighty bad when their scholars misses any p'int in public.

Well, sir, he took so long that d'reckly everybody begin to git wo'e out, an' at last Sonny, why, he got tired, too, an' he up an' says, says he, "Ef you can't make up your mind what to ask me, teacher, why 'n't you let me ask myself questions? An' ef my questions seem too easy, why, I'll put 'em to the class."

An', sir, with that he thess turns round, an' he says, says he, "Sonny Jones," says he, addressin' hisself, "what's the cause of total eclipses of the sun?" Thess that a-way he said it; an' then he turned around, an' he says, says he:

"Is that a hard enough question?"

"Very good," says teacher.

An', with that, Sonny he up an' picks up a' orange an' a' apple off the teacher's desk, an' says he, "This orange is the earth, an' this here apple is the sun." An', with that, he explained all they is to total eclipses. I can't begin to tell you thess how he expressed it, because I ain't highly edjercated myself, an' I don't know the specifactions. But when he had got thoo, he turned to the teacher, an' says he, "Is they anything else thet you'd like to know about total eclipses?" An' teacher says, says he, "Oh, no; not at all."

'This orange is the Earth, an' this here apple is the Sun.'
'This orange is the Earth, an' this here apple is the Sun.'
They do say thet them graduates hadn't never went so far ez total eclipses, an' teacher wouldn't 'a' had the subject mentioned to 'em for nothin'; but I don't say that's so.

Well, then, Sonny he turned around, an' looked at the company, an' he says, "Is everybody satisfied?" An' all the mothers an' fathers nodded their heads "yes."

An' then he waited thess a minute, an' he says, says he, "Well, now I'll put the next question:

"Sonny Jones," says he, "what is the difference between dew an' rain an' fog an' hail an' sleet an' snow!

"Is that a hard enough question?"

Well, from that he started in, an' he didn't stop tell he had expounded about every kind of dampness that ever descended from heaven or rose from the earth. An' after that, why, he went on a-givin' out one question after another, an' answerin 'em, tell everybody had declared theirselves entirely satisfied that he was fully equipped to gradj'ate—an', tell the truth, I don't doubt thet a heap of 'em felt their minds considerably relieved to have it safe-t over with without puttin' their grad'jates to shame, when what does he do but say, "Well, ef you're satisfied, why, I am—an' yet," says he, "I think I would like to ask myself one or two hard questions more, thess to make shore." An' befo' anybody could stop him, he had said:

"Sonny Jones, what is the reason thet a bird has feathers and a dog has hair?" An' then he turned around deliberate, an' answered: "I don't know. Teacher, please put that question to the class."

Teacher had kep' his temper purty well up to this time, but I see he was mad now, an' he riz from his chair, an' says he: "This examination has been declared finished, an' I think we have spent ez much time on it ez we can spare." An' all the mothers they nodded their heads, an' started a-whisperin'— most impolite.

An' at that, Sonny, why, he thess set down as modest an' peaceable ez anything; but ez he was settin' he remarked that he was in hopes thet some o' the reg'lars would 'a' took time to answer a few questions thet had bothered his mind f'om time to time—an' of c'ose they must know; which, to my mind, was the modes'est remark a boy ever did make.

Well, sir, that's the way this diplomy was earned—by a good, hard struggle, in open daylight, by unanymous vote of all concerned—an' unconcerned, for that matter. An' my opinion is thet if they are those who have any private opinions about it, an' they didn't express 'em that day, why they ain't got no right to do it underhanded, ez I am sorry to say has been done.

But it's his diplomy, an' it's handsomer fixed up than any in town, an' I doubt ef they ever was one anywhere thet was took more paternal pride in.

Wife she ain't got so yet thet she can look at it without sort o' cryin'—thess the look of it seems to bring back the figure o' the little feller, ez he helt his ground, single-handed, at that gradj'atin' that day.

Well, sir, we was so pleased to have him turned out a full gradj'ate thet, after it was all over, why, I riz up then and there, though I couldn't hardly speak for the lump in my th'oat, an' I said thet I wanted to announce thet Sonny was goin' to have a gradj'atin' party out at our farm that day week, an' thet the present company was all invited.

An' he did have it, too; an' they all come, every mother's son of 'em—from a to izzard—even to them that has expressed secret dissatisfactions; which they was all welcome, though it does seem to me thet, ef I 'd been in their places, I'd 'a' hardly had the face to come an' talk, too.

I'm this kind of a disposition myself: ef I was ever to go to any kind of a collation thet I expressed disapproval of, why, the supper couldn't be good enough not to choke me.

An' Sonny, why, he's constructed on the same plan. We ain't never told him of any o' the remarks thet has been passed. They might git his little feelin's hurted, an' 't wouldn't do no good, though some few has been made to his face by one or two smarty, ill-raised boys.

Well, sir, we give 'em a fine party, ef I do say it myself, an' they all had a good time. Wife she whipped up eggs an' sugar for a week befo'hand, an' we set the table out under the mulberries. It took eleven little niggers to wait on 'em, not countin' them thet worked the fly-fans. An' Sonny he ast the blessin'.

Then, after they'd all et, Sonny he had a' exhibition of his little specimens. He showed 'em his bird eggs, an' his wood samples, an' his stamp album, an' his scroll-sawed things, an' his clay-moldin's, an' all his little menagerie of animals an' things. I rather think everybody was struck when they found thet Sonny knowed the botanical names of every one of the animals he's ever tamed, an' every bird. Miss Phoebe, she didn't come to the front much. She stayed along with wife, an' helped 'tend to the company, but I could see she looked on with pride; an' I don't want nothin' said about it, but the boa'd of school directors was so took with the things she had taught Sonny thet, when the evenin' was over, they ast her to accept a situation in the academy next year, an' she's goin' to take it.

An' she says thet ef Sonny will take a private co'se of instruction in nachel sciences, an' go to a few lectures, why, th' ain't nobody on earth that she 'd ruther see come into that academy ez teacher,—that is, of co'se, in time. But I doubt ef he'd ever keer for it.

I've always thought thet school-teachin', to be a success, has to run in families, same ez anythin' else—yet, th' ain't no tellin'.

I don't keer what he settles on when he's grown; I expect to take pride in the way he'll do it—an' that's the principal thing, after all.

It's the "Well done" we're all a-hopin' to hear at the last day; an' the po' laborer thet digs a good ditch'll have thess ez good a chance to hear it ez the man that owns the farm.

Hello, doc'; come in! Don't ask me to shake hands, though; 't least, not tell I can drop this 'ere piece o' ribbin.

I never reelized how much shenanigan it took to tie a bow o' ribbin tell I started experimentin' with this here buggy-whup o' Sonny's.

An' he wants it tied thess so. He's a reg'lar Miss Nancy, come to taste.

All the boys, nowadays, they seem to think thet ez soon ez they commence to keep company, they must have ribbin bows tied on their buggy-whups—an' I reckon it's in accordance, ef anything is. I thess called you in to look at his new buggy, doctor. You've had your first innin's, ez the base-ball fellers says, at all o' his various an' sundry celebrations, from his first appearance to his gradj'atin', and I'll call your attention to a thing I wouldn't mention to a' outsider.

Sence he taken a notion to take the girls out a-ridin', why, I intend for him to do it in proper style; an' I went an' selected this buggy myself.

It is sort o' fancy, maybe, for the country, but I knew he'd like it fancy—at his age. I got it good an' high, so's it could straddle stumps good. They's so many tree-stumps in our woods, an' I know Sonny ain't a-goin' to drive nowhere but in the woods so long ez they's a livin' thin' to scurry away at his approach, or a flower left in bloom, or a last year's bird's nest to gether. An' the little Sweetheart, why, she's got so thet she's ez anxious to fetch home things to study over ez he is.

Yas; I think it is, ez you say, a fus'-class little buggy.

Sonny ain't never did nothin' half-ways,—not even mischief,—an' I ain't a-goin' in, at this stage o' his raisin', to stint him.

List'n at me sayin' "raisin'" ag'in, after all Miss Phoebe has preached to me about it! She claims thet folks has to be fetched up,—or "brung up" I believe she calls it,—an' I don't doubt she knows.

She allows thet pigs is raised, an' potaters, an' even chickens; an' she said, one day, thet ef I insisted on "raisin'" child'en, she'd raise a row. She's a quick hand to turn a joke, Miss Phoebe is.

Nobody thet ever lived in Simpkinsville would claim thet rows couldn't be raised, I'm shore, after all the fuss thet's been made over puttin' daytime candles in our 'piscopal church. Funny how folks'll fuss about sech a little thing when, ef they'd stop to think, they's so many mo' important subjec's thet they could git up diffe'nces of opinion on.

I didn't see no partic'lar use in lightin' the candles myself, bein' ez we didn't need 'em to see by, an' shorely the good Lord thet can speak out a sun any time he needs a extry taper couldn't be said to take no pleasure in a Simpkinsville home-dipped candle. But the way I look at it, seem like ef some wants em, why not?

Th' ain't nothin' mo' innercent than a lighted candle,—kep' away up on the wall out o' the draft, the way they are in church,—an' so, when it come to votin' on it, why, I count peace an' good-will so far ahead o' taller thet I voted thet I was good for ez many candles ez any other man would give. An' quick ez I said them words, why, Enoch Johnson up an' doubled his number. It tickled me to see him do it, too.

Enoch hates me thess because he's got a stupid boy—like ez ef that was any o' my fault. His Sam failed to pass at the preliminar' examination, an' wasn't allowed to try for a diplomy in public; an' Enoch an' his wife, why, they seem to hold it ag'in' me thet Sonny could step in at the last moment an' take what their boy could n't git th'oo the trials an' tribulations of a whole year o' bein' teached lessons at home an' wrestled in prayer over.

I ain't got a thing ag'in' Enoch, not a thing—not even for makin' me double my number o' candles. Mo' 'n that, I'd brighten up Sam's mind for 'im in a minute, ef I could.

I never was jealous-hearted. An' neither is Sonny.

He sent Sam a special invite to his gradj'atin' party, an' give him a seat next to hisself so's he could say "Amen" to his blessin', thess because he had missed gittin' his diplomy. Everybody there knowed why he done it.

But talkin' about Sonny being "raised," I told Miss Phoebe thet we'd haf to stop sayin' it about him, right or wrong, ez a person can't raise nothin' higher 'n what he is hisself, an Sonny's taller 'n either wife or me, an' he ain't but sixteen. Ef we raised 'im partly, we must 'a' sent 'im up the rest o' the way. It's a pleasure to pass a little joke with Miss Phoebe; she's got sech a good ear to ketch their p'ints.

But, come to growin', Sonny never asked nobody no odds. He thess stayed stock-still ez long ez he found pleasure in bein' a little runt, an' then he humped hisself an' shot up same ez a sparrer-grass stalk. It gives me pleasure to look up to him the way I haf to.

Fact is, he always did require me to look up to 'im, even when I looked down at 'im.

Yas, sir; ez I said, Sonny has commenced keepin' company,—outspoke,—an' I can't say thet I'm opposed to it, though some would say he was a little young, maybe. I know when I was his age I had been in love sev'al times. Of co'se these first little puppy-dog loves, why, th' ain't no partic'lar harm in 'em—less'n they're opposed.

An' we don't lay out to oppose Sonny—not in nothin' thet he'll attemp'—after him bein' raised an' guided up to this age.

There goes that word "raisin'" agi'n.

He's been in love with his teacher, Miss Phoebe, most three years—an' 'cep'n' thet I had a sim'lar experience when I was sca'cely out o' the cradle, why, I might 'a' took it mo' serious.

That sort o' fallin' in love, why, it comes same ez the measles or the two-year-old teeth, an' th' ain't nothin' sweeter ef it's took philosophical.

It's mighty hard, though, for parents, thet knows thess how recent a child is, to reconcile the facts o' the case with sech things ez him takin' notice to the color o' ribbin on a middle-aged school-teacher's hair—an' it sprinkled with gray.

Sonny was worse plegged than most boys, because, havin' two lady teachers at that time, it took him sort o' duplicated like.

I suppose ef he'd had another, he'd 'a' been equally distributed on all three.

The way I look at it, a sensible, serious-minded woman thet starts out to teach school—which little fellers they ain't got no sense on earth, nohow—ain't got no business with ribbin-bows an' ways an' moles on their cheek-bones. An' ef they've got knuckles, they ought to be like wife's or mine, pointed outward for useful service, instid o' bein' turned inside out to attract a young child's admiration—not thet I hold it against Miss Phoebe thet her knuckles is reversed. Of co'se she can't be very strong-fingered. No finger could git much purchase on a dimple.

'T ain't none of her fault, I know. But Sonny has seen the day thet seem like he couldn't talk about another thing but her an' her dimpled knuckles—them an' that little brown mole thet sets out on the aidge of her eyebrow.

I think myself thet that mole looks right well, for a blemish, which wife says it is, worst kind. But of co'se a child couldn't be expected to know that. It did seem a redic'lous part o' speech the first time he mentioned sech a thing to his mother, but a boy o' twelve couldn't be expected to know the difference between a mountain an' a mole-hill.

I ricollec' he used to talk in his sleep consider'ble when he was a little chap, an' it always fretted wife turrible. She'd git up out o' bed thess ez soon ez he'd begin to hold fo'th, an' taller him over. Whenever she didn't seem to know what else to do, why, she'd taller him; an' I don't reckon there's anything less injurious to a child, asleep or awake, than taller.

She's tallored him for his long division, an' she's tallered him for that blemish on Miss Phoebe's cheek, an' she's tallered him for clairin' of his th'oat. His other lady teacher, Miss Alviry Sawyer, she was a single-handed maiden lady long'bout wife's age, an' she didn't have a feature on earth thet a friend would seem to have a right to mention, she not bein' to blame; but she had a way o' clairin' her th'oat, sort o' polite, befo' she'd open her mouth to speak. Sonny, he seemed to think it was mighty graceful the way she done it, an' he's often imitated it in his little sleep—nights when he'd eat hot waffles for his supper.

An' wife she'd always jump up an' git the mutton taller. I never took it serious myself, 'cause I know how a triflin' thing 'll sometimes turn a level-headed little chap into a drizzlin' ejiot. I been there myself.

But th' ain't no danger in it, not less'n he's made a laughin'-stalk of—which is cruelty to animals, an' shouldn't be allowed.

I know when I went to school up here at Sandy Cri'k, forty year ago, I was teached by a certain single lady that has subsequently died a nachel death of old age an' virtuous works, an' in them days she wo'e a knitted collar, an' long curls both sides of her face; an' I've seen many a night, after the candle was out, thet she'd appear befo' me. She'd seem to come an' hang over my bed-canopy same ez a chandelier, with them side curls all a-jinglin' like cut-glass dangles. It's true, she used mostly to appear with a long peach-switch in her hand, but that was nachel enough, that bein' the way she most gen'ally approached me in life.

But of co'se I come th'oo without taller. My mother had thirteen of us, an' ef she'd started anointin' us for all our little side-curled nightmares, she'd 'a' had to go to goose raisin'.

You see, in them days they used goose grease.

I never to say admired that side-curled lady much, though she's made some lastin' impressions on me. Why, I could set down now, an' make a drawin' of that knitted collar she used to wear, an' it over forty year ago. I ricollec' she was cross-eyed, too, in the eye todes the foot o' the class, where I'd occasionally set; an', tell the truth, it was the strongest reason for study thet I had—thess to get on to the side of her certain eye. Th' ain't anything much mo' tantalizin' to a person than uncertainty in sech matters.

She was mighty plain, an' yet some o' the boys seemed to see beauty in her. I know my brother Bob, he confided to mother once-t thet he thought she looked thess precizely like the Queen o' Sheba must'a' looked, an' I ricollec' thet he cried bitter because mother told it out on him at the dinner-table. It was turrible cruel, but she didn't reelize.

I reckon, ef the truth was known, most of us nine has seen them side curls in our sleep. An' nobody but God an' his angels will ever know how many of us passed th'oo the valley o' the shadder o' that singular-appearin' lady, or how often we notified the other eight of the fact, unbeknowinst to his audience, while they was distributed in their little trundle-beds.

I sometimes wonder ef they ain't no account took of little child'en's trials. Seems to me they ought to be a little heavenly book kep' a-purpose; an' 't wouldn't do no harm ef earthly fathers an' mothers was occasionally allowed to look over it.

My brother Bob, him thet likened Miss Alviry to the Queen o' Sheba, always was a sensitive-minded child, an' we all knowed it, too; and yet, we never called him a thing for months after that but Solomon. We ought to've been whupped good for it.

Bob ain't never married, an' for a bachelor person of singular habits, he's kep' ez warm a heart ez ever I see.

I've often deplo'ed him not marryin'. In fact, sense I see what comfort is to be took in a child, why, I deplo' all the singular numbers—though the Lord couldn't be expected to have a supply on hand thess like Sonny to distribute 'round on demand.

But I doubt ef parents knows the difference.

I've noticed thet when they can't take pleasure in extry smartness in a child, why, they make it up in tracin' resemblances. I suppose they's parental comfort to be took to in all kinds o' babies. I know I've seen some dull-eyed ones thet seemed like ez ef they wasn't nothin' for 'em to do but resemble.

But talkin' about Sonny a-fallin' in love with his teachers, why, they was a time here when he wanted to give away every thing in the house to first one an' then the other. The first we noticed of it was him tellin' us how nice Miss Alviry thought his livers and gizzards was. Now, everybody knows thet they ain't been a chicken thet has died for our nourishment sence Sonny has cut his eye-teeth but has give up its vitals to him, an' give 'em willin'ly, they bein' the parts of his choice; an' it was discouragin', after killin' a useless number o' chickens to git enough to pack his little lunch-bucket, to have her eat 'em up—an' she forty year old ef she's a day, an' he not got his growth yet. An' yet, a chicken liver is thess one o' them little things thet a person couldn't hardly th'ow up to a school-teacher 'thout seemin' small-minded.

I never did make no open objection to him givin' away anything to his teachers tell the time he taken a notion to give Miss Phoebe the plush album out o' the parlor. We was buyin' it on instalments at twenty-five cents a week, and it wasn't fully installed at the time, an' I told him it wouldn't never do to give away what wasn't ours.

When it comes to principle, why, I always take a stand. I thought likely by the time it was ours in full he'd've recovered from his attackt, an' be willin' for his ma to keep it; an' he was.

An' besides, sence his pet squir'l has done chawed the plush clean off one corner of it, he says he wouldn't part with it for nothin'. Of co'se a beast couldn't be expected to reelize the importance o' plush. An' that's what seems to tickle Sonny so.

We had bought it chiefly on his account, so ez to git 'im accustomed to seein' handsome things around, so thet when he goes out into the world he won't need to be flustered by finery.

Wife she's been layin' by egg money all spring to buy a swingin', silver-plated ice-pitcher, so he'll feel at home with sech things, an' capable of walkin' up to one an' tiltin' it unconcerned, which is more'n I can do to this day. I always feel like ez ef I ought to go home an' put on my Sunday clo'es befo' I can approach one of 'em.

Sech ez that has to be worked into a person's constitution in youth. The motions of a gourd-dipper, kep' in constant practice for years, is mighty hard to reverse.

How does that look now, doctor? Yas; I think so, too. It's tied in a right good bow for a ten-thumbed man, which I shorely am, come to fingerin' ribbin.

He chose blue because she's got blue eyes—pore little human! Sir? Who is she, you say? Why, don't you know? She's Joe Wallace's little Mary Elizabeth—a nice, well-mannered child ez ever lived.

'What could be sweeter 'n little Mary Elizabeth?'
'What could be sweeter 'n little Mary Elizabeth?'
Wife has had her over here to supper sev'al nights lately, an' Sonny he's took tea over to the Wallaces' once-t or twice-t, an' they say he shows mighty good table manners, passin' things polite, an' leavin' proper amounts on his plate. His mother has always teached him keerful. It's good practice for 'em both. Of co'se Mary Elizabeth she's a year older 'n what Sonny is, an' she's thess gittin'

a little experience out o' him—though she ain't no ways conscious of it,—an' he 'll gain a good deal o' courage th'oo keepin' company with a ladylike girl like Mary Elizabeth. That's the way it goes, an' I think th' ain't nothin' mo' innercent or sweet.

How'd you say that, doctor? S'posin' it wasn't to turn out that-a-way? Well, bless yo' heart, ef it was to work out in all seriousness, what could be sweeter 'n little Mary Elizabeth? Sonny ain't got it in his power to displease us, don't keer what he was to take a notion to, less'n, of co'se, it was wrong, which it ain't in him to do—not knowin'ly.

You know, Sonny has about decided to take a trip north, doctor—to New York State. Sir? Oh, no; he ain't goin' to take the co'se o' lectures thet Miss Phoebe has urged him to take—'t least, that ain't his intention.

No; he sez thet he don't crave to fit his-self to teach. He sez he feels like ez ef it would smother him to teach school in a house all day. He taken that after me.

No; he's goin a-visitin'. Oh, no, sir; we ain't got no New York kin. He's a-goin' all the way to that strange an' distant State to call on a man thet he ain't never see, nor any of his family. He's a gentle man by the name o' Burroughs—John Burroughs. He's a book-writer. The first book thet Sonny set up nights to read was one o' his'n—all about dumb creatures an' birds. Sonny acchilly wo'e that book out a-readin' it.

Yas, sir; Sonny says thet ef he could thess take one long stroll th'oo the woods with him, he'd be willin' to walk to New York State if necessary. An' we're a-goin' to let 'im go. The purtiest part about it is thet this here great book-writer has invited him to pay him a visit. Think o' that, will you? Think of a man thet could think up a whole row o' books a-takin' sech a' int'res' in our plain little Arkansas Sonny. But he done it; an' 'mo' 'n that, he remarked in the letter thet it would give him great pleasure to meet the boy thet had so many mutual friends in common with him, or some sech remark. Of co'se, in this he referred to dumb brutes, an' even trees, so Sonny says. Oh, cert'n'y; Sonny writ him first. How would he've knew about Sonny? Miss Phoebe she encouraged him to write the letter, but it was Sonny's first idee. An' the answer, why, he's got it framed an' hung up above his bookshelves between our marriage c'tif'cate an' his diplomy.

He's done sent Sonny his picture, too. He's took a-settin' up in a' apple-tree.
You can tell from a little thing like that thet a person ain't no dude, an' I like
that. We 've put that picture in the front page of the plush album, an' moved
the bishop back one page.

Sonny has sent him a photograph of all our family took together, an' likely
enough he'll have it framed time Sonny arrives there.

When he goes, little Mary Elizabeth, why, she's offered to take keer of all his
harmless live things till he comes back, an' I s'pose they'll be letters a-passin'
back and fo'th. It does seem so funny, when I think about it. 'Pears like thess
the other day thet Mis' Wallace fetched little Mary Elizabeth over to look at
Sonny, an' he on'y three days old. I ricollec' when she seen 'im she took her
little one-year-old finger an' teched 'im on the forehead, an' she says, says she,
"Howdy?"—thess that-a-way. I remember we all thought it was so smart.
Seemed like ez ef she reelized thet he had thess arrived—an' she had thess
learned to say "Howdy," an' she up an' says it.

An' she's ap' at speech yet, so Sonny says. She don't say much when wife or I
are around, which I think is showin' only right an' proper respec's.

Th' ain't nothin' purtier, to my mind, than for a young girl to set up at table
with her elders, an' to 'tend strictly to business. Mary Elizabeth'll set th'oo a
whole meal, an' sca'cely look up from her plate. I never did see a little girl do it
mo' modest.

Of co'se, Sonny, he bein' at home, an' she bein' his company, why, he talks
constant, an' she'll glance up at him sort o' sideways occasional. Wife an' me,
we find it ez much ez we can do, sometimes, to hold in; we feel so tickled over
their cunnin' little ways together. To see Sonny politely take her cup o' tea an'
po' it out in her saucer to cool for her so nice, why, it takes all the dignity we
can put on to cover our amusement over it. You see, they've only lately teethed
together, them child'en.

I reckon the thing sort o' got started last summer. I know he give her a flyin'
squir'l, an' she embroidered him a hat-band. I suspicioned then what was
comin', an' I advised wife to make up a few white-bosomed shirts for him, an'
she didn't git 'em done none too soon. 'Twasn't no time befo' he called for 'em.

A while back befo' that I taken notice thet he 'd put a few idees down on sheets
o' paper for her to write her compositions by. Of co'se, he wouldn't write 'em.
He's too honest. He'd thess sugges' idees promiscu'us.

She's got words, so he says, an' so she'd write out mighty nice compositions by
his hints. I taken notice thet in this world it's often that-a-way; one'll have
idees, an' another'll have words. They ain't always bestowed together. When
they are, why, then, I reckon, them are the book-writers. Sonny he's got purty
consider'ble o' both for his age, but, of co'se, he wouldn't never aspire to put
nothin' he could think up into no printed book, I don't reckon; though he's got
three blank books filled with the routine of "out-door housekeeping," ez he calls
it, the way it's kep' by varmints an' things out o' doors under loose tree-barks
an' in all sorts of outlandish places. I did only last week find a piece o' paper
with a po'try verse on it in his hand-write on his little table. I suspicioned thet
it was his composin', because the name "Mary Elizabeth" occurred in two
places in it, though, of co'se, they's other Mary Elizabeths. He's a goin' to fetch
that housekeepin' book up north with him, an' my opinion is thet he's a-
projec'ing to show it to Mr. Burroughs. But likely he won't have the courage.

Yas; take it all together, I'm glad them two child'en has took the notion. It'll be
a good thing for him whilst he's throwed in with all sorts o' travelin' folks goin'
an' comin' to reelize thet he's got a little sweetheart at home, an' thet she's bein'
loved an' cherished by his father an' mother du'in' his absence.

Even after they've gone their sep'rate ways, ez they most likely will in time, it'll
be a pleasure to 'em to look back to the time when they was little sweethearts.

I know I had a number, off an' on, when I was a youngster, an' they're every
one hung up—in my mind, of co'se—in little gilt frames, each one to herself. An'
sometimes, when I think 'em over, I imagine thet they's sweet, bunches of wild
vi'lets a-settin' under every one of 'em—all 'cep'n' one, an' I always seem to see
pinks under hers.

An' she's a grandmother now. Funny to think it all over, ain't it? At this present
time she's a tall, thin ol' lady thet fans with a turkey-tail, an' sets up with the
sick. But the way she hangs in her little frame in my mind, she's a chunky
little thing with fat ankles an' wrisses, an' her two cheeks they hang out of her
pink caliker sunbonnet thess like a pair o' ripe plumgranates.

She was the pinkest little sweetheart thet a pink-lovin' school-boy ever picked out of a class of thirty-five, I reckon.

Seemed to me everything about her was fat an' chubby, thess like herself. Ricollec', one day, she dropped her satchel, an' out rolled the fattest little dictionary I ever see, an' when I see it, seem like she couldn't nachelly be expected to tote no other kind. I used to take pleasure in getherin' a pink out o' mother's garden in the mornin's when I'd be startin' to school, an' slippin' it on to her desk when she wouldn't be lookin', an' she'd always pin it on her frock when I'd have my head turned the other way. Then when she'd ketch my eye, she'd turn pinker'n the pink. But she never mentioned one o' them pinks to me in her life, nor I to her.

Yas; I always think of her little picture with a bunch o' them old-fashioned garden pinks a settin' under it, an' there they'll stay ez long ez my old mind is a fitten place for sech sweet-scented pictures to hang in.

They've been a pleasure to me all my life, an' I'm glad to see Sonny's a-startin' his little picture-gallery a'ready.

WEDDIN' PRESENTS

That you, doctor? Hitch up, an' come right in.

You say Sonny called by an' ast you to drop in to see me?

But I ain't sick. I'm thess settin'out here on the po'ch, upholstered with pillers this-a-way on account o' the spine o' my back feelin' sort o' porely. The way I ache—I reckon likely ez not it's a-fixin' to rain. Ef I don't seem to him quite ez chirpy I ought to be, why Sonny he gets oneasy an' goes for you, an' when I object—not thet I ain't always glad to see you, doctor—why, he th'ows up to me thet that's the way we always done about him when de was in his first childhood. An' ef you ricollec'—why, it's about true. He says he's boss now, an' turn about is fair play.

My pulse ain't no ways discordant, is it? No, I thought not. Of co'se, ez you say, I s'pose it's sort o' different to a younger person's, an' then I've been so worked up lately thet my heart's bound to be more or less frustrated, and Sonny says a person's heart reg'lates his pulse.

I reckon I ain't ez strong ez I ought to be, maybe, or I wouldn't cry so easy ez what I do. I been settin' here, pretty near boo-hoo-in' for the last half-hour, over the weddin' presents Sonny has thess been a-givin' me.

Last week it was a daughter, little Mary Elizabeth—an' now it's his book.

They was to 've come together. The book was printed and was to 've been received here on Sonny's weddin'-day, but it didn't git in on time. But I counted it in ez one o' my weddin' presents from Sonny, give to me on the occasion of his marriage, thess the same, though I didn't know about the inscription thet he's inscribed inside it tell it arrived—an' I'm glad I didn't.

Ef I'd 've knew that day, when my heart was already in my win'-pipe, thet he had give out to the world by sech a printed declaration ez that thet he had to say dedicated all his work in life, in advance, to my ol' soul, I couldn't no mo' 've kep' up my behavior 'n nothin'.

I'm glad you think I don't need no physic, doctor. I never was no hand to swaller medicine when I was young, and the obnoxion seems to grow on me ez I git older.

Not all that toddy? You'll have me in a drunkard's grave yet,—you an' Sonny together,—ef I don't watch out.

That nutmeg gives it a mighty good flavor, doc'. Ef any thing ever does make me intemp'rate, why, it'll be the nutmeg an' sugar thet you all smuggle the liquor to me in.

It does make me see clairer, I vow it does, either the nutmeg or the sperit, one.

There's Sonny's step, now. I can tell it quick ez he sets it on the back steps. Sence I'm sort o' laid up, Sonny gits into the saddle every day an' rides over the place an' gives orders for me.

Come out here, son, an' shake hands with the doctor.

Pretty warm, you say it is, son! An' th' ain't nothin' goin' astray on the place? Well, that's good. An', doc', here, he says thet his bill for this visit is a unwarranted extravagance 'cause they ain't a thing I need but to start on the downward way thet leads to ruin. He's got me all threatened with the tremens now, so thet I hardly know how to match my pronouns to suit their genders an' persons. He's give me fully a tablespoonful o' the reverend stuff in one toddy. I tell him he must write out a prescription for the gold cure an' leave it with me, so's in case he should drop off befo' I need it, I could git it, 'thout applyin' to a strange doctor an' disgracin' everybody in America by the name o' Jones.

Do you notice how strong he favors her to-day, doctor?

I don't know whether it's the toddy I've took thet calls my attention to it or not.

'When I set here by myself on this po'ch so much these days an' think.'
'When I set here by myself on this po'ch so much these days an' think.'
She always seemed to see me in him—but I never could. Far ez I can see, he never taken nothin' from me but his sect—an' yo' name, son, of co'se. 'Cep'in' for me, you couldn't 'a' been no Jones—'t least not in our branch.

Put yo' hand on my forr'd, son, an' bresh it up'ards a few times, while I shet my eyes.

Do you know when he does that, doc', I couldn't tell his hand from hers.

He taken his touch after her, exact—an' his hands, too, sech good firm fingers, not all plowed out o' shape, like mine. I never seemed to reelize it tell she'd passed away.

That'll do now, boy. I know you want to go in an' see where the little wife is, an' I've no doubt you'll find her with a wishful look in her eyes, wonderin' what keeps you out here so long.

Funny, doctor, how seein' him and little Mary Elizabeth together brings back my own youth to me—an' wife's.

From the first day we was married to the day we laid her away under the poplars, the first thing I done on enterin' the house was to wonder where she was an' go an' find her. An' quick ez I'd git her located, why, I'd feel sort o' rested, an' know things was all right.

Heap of his ma's ways I seem to see in Sonny since she's went.

An' what do you think, doc'? He's took to kissin' me nights and mornin's since she's passed away, an' I couldn't tell you how it seems to comfort me.

Maybe that sounds strange to you in a grown-up man, but it don't come no ways strange to me—not from Sonny. Now he's started it, seems like ez ef I'd 've missed it if he hadn't.

Ez I look back, they ain't no lovin' way thet a boy could have thet ain't seemed to come nachel to him—not a one. An' his little wife, Mary Elizabeth, why, they never was a sweeter daughter on earth.

An' ef I do say it ez shouldn't, their weddin' was the purtiest thet has ever took place in this county—in my ricollection, which goes back distinc' for over sixty year.

Everybody loves little Mary Elizabeth, an' th' aint a man, woman, or child in the place but doted on Sonny, even befo' he turned into a book-writer. But, of co'se, all the great honors they laid on him—the weddin' supper an' dance in the Simpkins's barn, the dec'rations o' the church that embraced so many things he's lectured about an' all that—why they was all meant to show fo'th how everybody took pride in him, ez a author o' printed books.

You see he has give' twelve lectures in the academy each term for the last three years, after studyin' them three winters in New York, each year's lectures different, but all relatin' to our own forests an' their dumb population. That's what he calls 'em. Th' ain't a boy thet has attended the academy, sence he's took the nachel history to teach, but'll tell you thess what kind o' inhabitants to look for on any particular tree. Nearly every boy in the county's got a cabinet—an' most of 'em have carpentered 'em theirselves, though I taught 'em how to do that after the pattern Sonny got me to make his by—an' you'll find all sorts o' specimens of what they designate ez "summer an' winter resorts" in pieces of bark an' cobweb an' ol' twisted tree-leaves in every one of 'em.

The boys thet dec'rated the barn for the dance say thet they ain't a tree Sonny ever lectured about but was represented in the ornaments tacked up ag'inst the wall, an' they wasn't a space big ez yo' hand, ez you know, doctor, thet wasn't covered with some sort o' evergreen or berry-branch, or somethin'.

An' have you heerd what the ol' nigger Proph' says? Of co'se he's all unhinged in the top story ez anybody would be thet lived in the woods an' e't sca'cely anything but herbs an' berries. But, anyhow, he's got a sort o' gift o' prophecy an' insight, ez we all know.

Well, Proph', he sez that while the weddin' march was bein' played in the church the night o' Sonny's weddin' thet he couldn't hear his own ears for the racket among all the live things in the woods. An' he says thet they wasn't a frog, or a cricket, or katydid, or nothin', but up an' played on its little instrument, an' thet every note they sounded fitted into the church music— even to the mockin'-bird an' the screech-owl.

Of co'se, I don't say it's so, but the ol' nigger swears to it, an' ef you dispute it with him an' ask him how it come thet nobody else didn't hear it, why he says that's because them thet live in houses an' eat flesh ain't got the love o' Grod in their hearts, an' can't expect to hear the songs of the songless an' speech of the speechless.

That's a toler'ble high-falutin figgur o' speech for a nigger, but it's thess the
way he expresses it.

You know he's been seen holdin' conversation with dumb brutes, more 'n once-
t—in broad daylight.

Of co'se, we can't be shore thet they was rejoicin' expressed in the underbrush
an' the forests, ez he says, but I do say, ez I said before, thet Sonny an' the
little girl has had the purtiest an' joyfulest weddin' I ever see in this county, an'
a good time was had by everybody present. An' it has made me mighty happy—
it an' its results.

They say a son is a son till he gets him a wife, but 't ain't so in this case, shore.
I've gained thess ez sweet a daughter ez I could 'a' picked out ef I'd 'a' had the
whole world to select from.

Little Mary Elizabeth has been mighty dear to our hearts for a long time, an'
when wife passed away, although the weddin' hadn't took place yet, she
bestowed a mother's partin' blessin' on her, an' give Sonny a lot o' private
advice about her disposition, an' how he ought to reg'late hisself to deal with it.

You see, Mary Elizabeth stayed along with us so much durin' the seasons he
was away in New York, thet we got to know all her crotchets an' quavers, an'
she ain't got a mean one, neither.

But they're there. An' they have to be dealt with, lovin'. Fact is, th' ain't no
other proper way to deal with nothin', in my opinion.

We was ruther glad to find out some little twists in her disposition, wife an' me
was, 'cause ef we hadn't discovered none, why we'd 'a' felt shore she had some
in'ard deceit or somethin'. No person can't be perfec', an' when I see people
always outwardly serene, I mistrust their insides.

But little Mary Elizabeth, why, she ain't none too angelic to git a good healthy
spell o' the pouts once-t in a while, but ef she's handled kind an' tender, why,
she'll come thoo without havin' to humble herself with apologies.

It depends largely upon how a pout is took, whether it'll contrac' itself into a
hard knot an' give trouble or thess loosen up into a good-natured smile, an' the
oftener they are let out that-a-way, the seldomer they'll come.

Little Mary Elizabeth, why, she looks so purty when she pouts, now, that I've been tempted sometimes to pervoke her to it, thess to witness the new set o' dimples she'll turn out on short notice; but I ain't never done it. I know a dimple thet's called into bein' too often in youth is li'ble to lay the foundation of a wrinkle in old age.

But takin' her right along stiddy, day in an' day out, she's got a good sunny disposition an' is mighty lovin' and kind.

An' as to character and dependableness, why, she's thess ez sound ez a bell.

In a heap o' ways she nears up to us, sech, f' instance, ez when she taken wife's cook-receipt book to go by in experimentin' with Sonny's likes an' dislikes. 'T ain't every new-married wife thet's willin' to sample her husband's tastes by his ma's cook-books.

They seem to think they 're too dictatorial.

But, of co'se, wife's receipts was better 'n most, an' Mary Elizabeth, she knows that.

She ain't been married but a week, but she's served up sev'al self-made dishes a'ready—all constructed accordin' to wife's schedule.

Of co'se I could see the diff'ence in the mixin'—but it only amused me. An' Sonny seemed to think thet, ef anything, they was better 'n they ever had been—which is only right and proper.

Three days after she was married, the po' little thing whipped up a b'iled custard for dinner an', some way or other, she put salt in it 'stid o' sugar, and poor Sonny—Well, I never have knew him to lie outright, befo', but he smacked his lips over it an' said it was the most delicious custard he had ever e't in his life, an' then, when he had done finished his first saucer an' said, "No, thank you, I won't choose any more," to a second helpin', why, she tasted it an' thess bust out a-cryin'.

But I reckon that was partly because she was sort o' on edge yet from the excitement of new housekeepin' and the head o' the table.

Well, I felt mighty sorry to see her in tears, an' what does Sonny do but insist on eatin' the whole dish o' custard, an' soon ez I could git a chance, I took him aside an' give him a little dose-t o' pain-killer, an' I took a few drops myself.

I had felt obligated to swaller a few spoonfuls o' the salted custard when she'd be lookin' my way, an' I felt like ez ef I was pizened, an' so I thess took the painkiller ez a sort o' anecdote.

Another way Mary Elizabeth shows sense is the way she accepts discipline from the ol' nigger, Dicey.

She's mighty old an' strenuous now, Dicey is, an' she thinks because she was present at Sonny's birth an' before it, thet she's privileged to correct him for anything he does, and we've always indulged her in it, an' thess ez soon as she knowed what was brewin' 'twix' him an' Mary Elizabeth, why, she took her into the same custody, an' it's too cute for anything the way the little girl takes a scoldin' from her—thess winkin' at Sonny an' me while she receives it.

An' the ol' nigger'd lay down her life for her most ez quick ez she would for Sonny.

She was the first to open our eyes to the state of affairs 'twixt the two child'en, that ol' nigger was. It was the first year Sonny went North. He had writ home to his ma from New York State, and said thet Mr. Burroughs had looked over his little writings an' said they was good enough to be printed an' bound up in a book.

Wife, she read the letter out loud, ez she always done, an' we noticed thet when we come to that, Mary Elizabeth slipped out o' the room; but we didn't think nothin' of it tell direc'ly ol' Dicey, she come in tickled all but to death to tell us thet the little girl was out on the po'ch with her face hid in the honeysuckle vines, cryin' thess ez hard as we was. So then, of co'se, we knowed that ef the co'se of true love could be allowed to run smooth for once-t, she was fo'-ordained to be our little blessin'—an' his—that is, so far as she was concerned.

Of co'se we was even a little tenderer todes her, after that, than we had been befo'.

That was over five year ago, an' th' ain't been a day sca'cely sence then but we've seen her, an' in my jedgment they won't be nothin' lackin' in her thet's needful in a little wife—not a thing.

Ef they's anything in long acquaintance, they've certainly knowed one another all the time they've had.

Of co'se Mary Elizabeth, she ain't to say got Sonny's thoughts, exac'ly, where it comes to sech a thing ez book-writin', but he says she's a heap better educated 'n what he is.

She's got all her tuition repo'ts du'in' the whole time she attended school, an' mostly all her precentages was up close onto the hund'eds.

Sonny never was no hand on earth to git good reports at school.

They was always so low down in figgurs thet he calls 'em his "misconduc' slips."

But they ain't a one he's ever got, takin' 'em from the beginnin' clean up to the day o' his gradjuatin', thet ain't got some lovin' remark inscribed acrost it from his teacher—not a one.

Even them that wrastled with him most severe has writ him down friendly an' kind.

An' little Mary Elizabeth—why, she's took every last one of 'em an' she's feather-stitched 'em aroun' the edges an' sewed 'em up into a sort o' little book, an' tied a ribbin' bow acrost it. I don't know whether she done it on account o' the teacher's remarks or not—but she cert'n'y does prize that pamphlet.

She thinks so much of it thet I been advisin' her to take out a fire insu'ance on it.

In a heap o' ways she thess perzacly suits Sonny. Lookin' at it from one p'int o' view, she's a sort o' dictionary to him.

Whenever Sonny finds hisself short of a date, f' instance, or some unreasonable spellin' 'll bother 'im, why, he'll apply to her for it an' she'll hand it out to him, intac'. I ain't never knew her to fail.

You see, while Sonny's thoughts is purty far-reachin' in some ways, he's received his education so sort o' hit an' miss thet the things he knows ain't to say catalogued in his mind, an' while he'll know one fac', maybe he won't be able to recall another thet seems to belong hand in hand with it. An' that's one reason why I say thet little Mary Elizabeth is thess the wife for him.

She may not bother about the whys an' wherefores, but she's got the statistics.

It's always well, in a married couple, to have either one or the other statistical, so thet any needed fac' can be had on demand.

Wife, she was a heap more gifted that-a-way 'n what I was, but of co'se hers wasn't so much book statistics.

She could give the name an' age of every cow an' calf on the farm, an' relate any circumstance thet has took place within her recollection or mine without the loss of a single date or any gain through imagination, either.

I don't know but I think that's a greater gif' than the other, to be able to reproduce a event after a long time without sort o' thess techin' it up with a little exaggeration.

Th' ain't no finer trait, in my opinion, in man or woman, than dependableness, an' that's another reason I take sech special delight in the little daughter, Mary Elizabeth.

If she tells you a thing's black, why you may know it don't lean todes brown or gray. It's thess a dismal black.

She may hate to say it, an' show her hatred in a dozen lovin', regretful ways, but out it'll come.

An' I think thet any man thet can count on a devoted wife for exactitude is blessed beyond common.

So many exac' women is col'-breasted an' severe. An' ef I had to take one or the other, why, I'd let my wife prevaricate a little, ef need be, befo' I'd relinquish warmheartedness, an' the power to command peacefulness an' rest, an' make things comfortable an' homely, day in an' day out.

Maybe I'm unprincipled in that, but life is so short, an' ef we didn't have lovin' ways to lengthen out our days, why I don't think I'd keer to bother with it, less'n, of co'se, I might be needful to somebody else.

Yas, doc', I 'm mighty happy in the little daughter—an' the book—an' the blessed boy hisself. Maybe I'm too talkative on the subject, but the way I feel about him, I might discuss him forever, an' then they'd be thess a little sweetness left over thet I couldn't put into words about him.

Not thet he's faultless. I don't suppose they ever was a boy on earth thet had mo' faults 'n Sonny, but they ain't one he's got thet I don't seem to cherish because I know it's rooted in honest soil.

You may strike a weed now an' ag'in, but he don't grow no pizen vines in his little wilderness o' short-comin's. Th' ain't no nettles in his garden o' faults. That ain't a bad figgur o' speech for a ol' man like me, is it, doctor?

But nex' time he stops an' tells you I'm sick, you thess tell him to go about his business.

I'm failin' in stren'th ez the days go—an' I know it—an' it's all right.

I don't ask no mo' 'n thess to pass on whenever the good Lord wills.

But of co'se I ain't in no hurry, an' they's one joy I'd like to feel befo' that time comes.

I'd love to hol' Sonny's baby in my ol' arms—his an' hers—an' to see thet the good ol' name o' Jones has had safe transportation into one mo' generation of honest folks.

Sonny an' Mary Elizabeth are too sweet-hearted an' true not to be reproduced in detail, an' passed along.

This here ol' oak tree thet gran'pa planted when I was a kid, why, it'd be a fine shady place for healthy girls an' boys to play under.

'Seem like a person don't no mo' 'n realize he's a descendant befo' he's a' ancestor.'

'Seem like a person don't no mo' 'n realize he's a descendant befo' he's a' ancestor.'
When I set here by myself on this po'ch so much these days an' think,—an' remember,—why I thess wonder over the passage o' time.

I ricollec' thess ez well when gran'pa planted that oak saplin'. My pa he helt it stiddy an' I handed gran'pa the spade, an' we took off our hats whilst he repeated a Bible tex'.

Yes, that ol' oak was religiously planted, an' we've tried not to offend its first principles in no ways du'in' the years we've nurtured it.

An' when I set here an' look at it, an' consider its propensities,—it's got five limbs that seem thess constructed to hold swings,—maybe it's 'cause I was raised Presbyterian an' sort o' can't git shet o' the doctrine o' predestination, but I can't help seemin' to fo'-see them friendly family limbs all fulfillin' their promises.

An' when I imagine myself a-settin' there with one little one a-climbin' over me while the rest swings away, why, seem like a person don't no mo' 'n realize he's a descendant befo' he's a' ancestor.